RAY D. HUGHES, M.D.

Poorboy at the Party

BY ROBERT GOVER

ONE HUNDRED DOLLAR MISUNDERSTANDING
and
HERE GOES KITTEN

THE MANIAC RESPONSIBLE

POORBOY AT THE PARTY

Robert Gover

TRIDENT PRESS   New York

1966

ACKNOWLEDGMENT: Samuel Goldwyn, Jr., without whose objection this novel would not have been written.

DEDICATION: For the people of Gifford, Fla., from whom the author was learning while he was at work on this novel.

Also for Lois, Scott Meredith, Herb Alexander, and Buck Moon; Abe Friedman and Ellis Freedman.

AUTHOR'S NOTE

Those who look forward to going to some Heaven up in the sky when they become bones and compost or atomized particles are kindly warned that they may find this novel unsatisfactory. It is, I hope, a novel of some hope for those who are made sick and wonderous by our species' peculiar instinct to ruin itself, for it makes an attempt—on a small scale and in its own unlikely way—to find out what they (we) are, and to separate a Them, an aspect of ourselves, from the rest of us.

Poorboy at the Party

1

I OFTEN MEET people who ask me why it happened. Who say they could understand kids from the slums behaving that way, but the sons and daughters of our best families—why them?

Well, I find that a funny question. And a bit dangerous. The kind who ask it usually think I'm somebody I'm not, really. They assume that since I was there the night it happened, and since I'm now a total and irrevocable dropout, beachboy, bum, beatnik, student of life—they assume I must be a fallen angel out of the overprivileged class. Which I'm not. Not by a long shot.

I'm poor dirtfarmer whitetrash with origins in the country slum and prep school in an orphanage. I went to the party as an outsider, the guest of a guy whose presence there was like an atmospheric pressure, and in some witch-crafty way, brought on the storm.

Or was it me who brought it on? No, no—to give credit where credit is due, it was Arnold, for even I was just another one of the ingredients he added to the party, and all I brought to it was my poorboy's spooky prejudice against the rich and powerful.

I was, really, the most non-active one there, the only

1

one who sat back and watched the big scene. Which, I figure, is what qualifies me to say that *why* it happened is anybody's unscrewable inscrutable to screw around with. I tend to feel it has something to do with a bigger why—why we humans seem so determined to destroy ourselves—but that's just another piece of the same old Chinese puzzle—and I leave it to minds more prone than mine to the fancies of syllogism, and to those tongues that lick so nicely over the many-syllabled surfaces of the psycho-analytical jargon.

As for *what* happened—now that's something else. That's the story I *can* tell. For me to tell it, though, I'll have to beg your indulgence about a couple of matters. Because, you see, my telling of it will go to some lengths to avoid the exact names of people and places; to do it any other way would only divert your attention and put you connecting certain members of that party with certain governors of our various states of pomp and chaos, the royalty of our Dupedoms, and that would cause to blur what I want my telling of it to focus on.

Because it serves my prejudice to forget those proper nouns, and I did, for a certain, go to that party with a definite, deep-rooted prejudice. I've been able to overcome it somewhat since then. Nowadays, I'm able to see the rich and powerful as a very large category which most of us fit into, one way or another. Health, beauty, knowledge, wisdom, spirit. There are many forms of wealth and some of the richest in stocks and real estate suffer malnutrition of the sensibilities.

But that doesn't change the fact that, back in those days, I thought of the rich and powerful as one big lumpen generality—like everybody who lives in a fashionable suburb—and they all looked as much alike to my eyes as Negroes do to some of them. So even though my skin is light, eyes are blue, hair is blond, there is considerable Negritude in the way I view them, the rich and powerful, and this is so because when they look at me and my kind they don't see what's really us; they see through the veils of the myths they've told themselves about us, and so the people they are seeing don't exist. They can't afford to see the reality, for it would shatter their collective dreamlife, yank the props out from under their pomposity, bring them down to earth.

As for my own prejudice and veil of myths, I still had fresh memories of sitting by the roadside watching them whizbang by in big expensive cars, or jetline away overhead. Of glimpsing them through the windows of fancy restaurants stuffing themselves full of what my old pappy had a habit of calling "our grub." Because, as he impressed upon my tender young mind, it was us poor people who had sweated, bled, even died to make things grow in this land, and when you make something out of your dreams and muscle and sweat, it belongs to you no matter what the law says, because the law is their way of swindling us out of it.

And so, you see, when one of them happened by, looking sympathetically down his benevolent nose at my tattered, tumbledown circumstances, it never failed to stir my juices; my childhood idea of Romance was to take back from them what they'd taken from us. Not to loosen their fists and make them share it, for in my fondest daydream I turned the tables on them completely and left

3

them nothing but their store-bought pretensions, their chin-up, pomp-assed, put-on airs.

For I'd been reared on tales of uncles who'd been Wobblies and got busted, and long before I heard the word "bourgeois" I knew as sure as sunrise that a fix was on to turn me into their gutless flunky; it didn't take Karl Marx to tell me that the rich get richer while the poor get poorer, I was born a-knowing. I knew, too, that they could bust me like they'd done all those others. And they would —unless I could fox them. And at one point in my life I got the wild idea that the best way to fox them would be to go straight up their silly social ladder and smack dab into their midst. I figured that would put me where I could play their game and then all I'd have to learn would be the groundrules and how much you can cheat without getting put away. I told myself that all they really had going for them was their conniving ways, their expert thievery and the fact that their law was made to protect them from the likes of me. And I felt that, being of the people who really own what they call theirs, the people they'd taken it from and put down and were now being so niggardly benevolent toward—being of these people gave me more grit and gumption than they dreamed of, and I felt that if I could infiltrate and get to play their game, I'd give them some big surprises.

The first to get a whiff of this half-baked ambition I carried was my good friend Arnold. And he, ironically enough, nurtured and cultivated it—though he never quite understood it—until he finally killed it with care. It was Arnold who took me to that party and it was there that it died, my ambition. Died and got buried in the realization

4

that my choices weren't as restricted as I'd thought, that it isn't a matter of either fox them or get busted by them. But that's another story—the Sermon on the Mount updated—and before I get sidetracked I'd better move along with this one, clue you in on Arnold and our most unusual friendship.

He has slightly Oriental eyes and wears a perpetual leer, and he looks, in the right light, like an Arab chieftain— lean, dark, taller than I. His mother is Jewish and his father Anglo-Saxon with an ambassadorship somewhere in his past, and the family has four houses here and there across the country.

We met during freshman registration. He was wandering around outside the building trying to get someone to carry his cards through that long line, and I took it on, going through once for myself and a second time as him. He'd hinted at a cash payment for this service, so that night I went to the address he'd given me to collect. Instead of handing me money, though, he invited me into his very posh pad and asked me to stay for dinner. I'd already had one dinner—my swimming scholarship bought that one in the university cafeteria—but such an invitation from one in such surroundings as these brought me on famished.

It was a memorable dinner. The first I'd ever had that began with cocktails, proceeded through wine and got topped off with orgasm—this tall, dark, princely looking character going stealthily down and, as they call it, violating my sex orally. I sat back in amazement, marveling at this stroke of good luck, encountering a rich faggot my first time out. But how such a character as this could be gay I couldn't figure—and he was just as baffled by my lack

5

of the usual red-blooded American inner conflicts and middleclass inhibitions. Back in the all-boys orphanage I was just out of, back before I knew there was a language for it, I'd been the love object and the lover in various homosexual affairs—had even made it with both genders and both races on certain very busy nights. Like the night I went AWOL to keep a date with a colored girl and go through a couple of positions with her in the dark under the stairs in her place, then went home by way of the Polish neighborhood where there was a woman with a notorious, voracious itch for teenaged boys, and arrived back in the dorm still moonstruck enough to hump one of the boys who'd assumed that role. By the time I was eighteen, I'd had clap twice and was looking for some new style of sexlife—a more hygienic, less frantic way.

Anyhow, the next day Arnold surprised me all over again—I met him coming up the walk with a chick in a skirt that just begged and hollered every move she made. There was another dinner that night and this time it was a threesome, and so began our friendship, me and this richboy who was making a campaign on the sort of promiscuity I'd grown up with. Well, it all seemed harmless to me then—since I'd not yet learned about human queenbees and the fate of their drones—and his booze was topshelf and plentiful, so I made my contributions to those scenes and quickly developed a sponge for scotch and was soon puking my guts out about every other day at swimming practice. But that seemed a small price to pay, for I fancied these scenes served my half-baked ambition to infiltrate the upper strata.

And another factor was that my background had not

6

prepared me for the university milieu. Not at all. For instance, the bullsessions: I found that half the things they talked about were over my head, and when they used certain phrases like "making out," they were talking about something else. When they got onto the subject of which girls did and which did not, I got chills and horrors in my stomach, because where I was from such a question would brand you as a dud. It was never, Will she or Won't she— it was, What will it take to make her. I found that university life wasn't what I'd thought it would be, and that it was beyond my meager social skills to cope with this respectable way of agonizing through seemingly endless and meaningless complexities to get to the plain old ordinary sexlife I felt was rightfully mine by the fact of my existence. It seemed like a conspiracy to cut off my balls and shut off my natural flow of gism, and it soon had me feeling like I'd been hexed and had a soul full of devils that were trying to drive me up the sides of walls. Besides, I wasn't a bit interested in any kind of academic achievement, for there was something about the assumptions and values their knowledge smelled of that repelled me, so my situation was fairly intolerable.

Arnold became my salvation from that insanity and the first thing I learned at the university was not to stray too far from his sphere of influence. In fact, I soon came to treasure my friendship with him like a newly converted Billy Graham follower treasures his conversion, and for the best part of three years I was his faithful following. This had its embarrassing moments, of course. Like the time he came to see the swimming meet. He wandered down to our bench to chat and I asked him what he thought of it, and he suddenly went swish and blurted out loud enough for the whole team to hear: "Oh, I *love* that distance freestyler, the one who came in last. Magnificent form!" Which my teammates never forgot.

But the compensations were too much—the apartment, the food and booze and the girls who damn well did, and six ways on Sunday. Every now and then we even managed a few who didn't. Arnold had a built-in, dream-reading radar, a way of cataloging and computing small slips of the tongue, reflexive actions, habits, mannerisms, and of intuiting the daydreams behind the priggish front, and we made quite a production out of helping such a chick convert it from her dreamlife to his bed—we tail-blazing pioneers in the virgin forests of innocence.

It didn't take him long to become disenchanted with me as a love object and we went on as friends, but through it all he never came off his faggotry. About which we soon developed a running argument. I maintained he faked it, that it was all a big put-on, and during our sophomore year I even doped out a reason. His father had fed him from an early age on tidbits about the superior individual —by which he meant the propertied class—a lot of crap about how he, the father, was a superior individual who had married a superior individual and sired superior individuals. When the young Arnold would go home—from whichever boarding school they'd stuck him in, to whichever house they were visiting at the time—it was to render a progress report to the commander in chief. Well, he cracked during his late teens and went on the couch with a shrink of the Karen Horney school of thought, who put the good word into his head that he should find himself, learn exactly who he is and is not, and not try to be somebody else. It developed that this psychoanalyst was gay and not at all sneaky about it, and Arnold found something to admire in this attitude. The upshot was, he decided to cultivate his own gay side. As a way to gain a clearer perspective on life, he said.

It was my contention, though, that his brand of gay was very grim. More like Napoleon's Russian campaign, the ultra egoist moving into territory that wasn't rightfully his. I used to tell him that he'd better get the hell out before it froze over and trapped him, and I used to ask him why he didn't save faggotry for his retirement years. But in his portfolio of rationalizations, it was not at all as I saw it; he claimed to have the best of both worlds—all the goodies of the straight, plus those unknown to the prude strapped by pride and fear, was his way of putting it. Besides, he used to say, you have your sport, swimming, so I have a right to mine, lechery.

And there was irony in that too—swimming being traditionally the sport of the well-to-do.

Anyhow, it wasn't until later that I came to see his bisexuality as a form of rebellion against the bloodless rigidities of his childhood and youth—those restraints that had been built into him as tightly as the involuntary activities of his digestive tract—and then I came to appreciate a certain courage he put into those grim forays on the gay, and to comprehend a little about what he got back.

So, maybe that gives you some idea of who we were when we went to that party. He, the assured and suave heir to oldmoney and social standing. Me, the offspring of those whose sweat and blood had been the making of that oldmoney, the support of that social standing. The handsome bisexual richboy from the four-house family and the socially backward poorboy from the two-seater outhouse family. And by this time we had in our past many an involved discussion about how I should—but not without his astute guidance—do what we called "catch a ride to the thin air," and do it by finding "a daughter of the newmoney who has those certain guilts you can husband, in return for which."

But our project never seemed to get off the ground. The trouble being that I always ended up feeling, when surrounded by the sons and daughters of the rich and powerful, like an English-speaking idiot studying metaphysics in Vienna. Or, like a spectator at a tennis match being played with invisible balls. Still, I had a purple-headed passion for richchicks and a sneaking suspicion that the times were ripe for the exploiteds to exploit the exploiters. For I'd been reduced to supposing I must either fight them or join them—infiltrate or get busted. Aspire to such glories as vice president in charge of cocktails or stroll through their corridors blowing pot. In short, I was a hesitant, blundering social climber.

2

IT WAS THE END of our junior year, the first Saturday after finals, and Arnold suggested we spend a few days at his family's mountain retreat, the only home he had that was in driving distance from the university. We'd spent other times there—fishing, hiking through the woods, going to sleep serenaded by that loud chorus of little creatures outside—and I was in a happy hurry that bright morning to stash my overnight bag in the trunk of his MG and be on our way. I never suspected he had a surprise up his sleeve. Or, to put it another way, he usually had something up his sleeve but I didn't look for anything so far out of his ordinary that day.

We put the top down and drove through the worst of the city traffic, then stopped at a drive-in liquor store. Out on the highway we sipped and sang—the songs from my childhood in the country slum intrigued him. Each time I'd remember another, I'd teach him the words and tune, and we'd sing it a few times with emphasis on the downhome dialect.

I guess I was too busy savoring "Barbry Allen" or something when he turned off the highway, for I was unaware we were making a detour. When I got with it, we were astride a humpbacked road through the wilds. Then we

11

were going through a wrought-iron gate overgrown with thick vines, into what looked for all the world like the abandoned country estate of yesteryear's biggest tycoon. And we were going downhill along the tree-lined drive of this place and the air was becoming delicious—the sea was in it and so was a perfumey mixture of early-summer flowers.

Suddenly there was a house—and what a house: three stories high and about as long as a downtown hotel. The windows were all boarded up, yet the lawn was trim as a golfing green. We turned the driveway and rolled to the front of this house, and here there were enough cars for a good-sized parking lot.

No use asking him what this detour was all about. The only way to get the straight scoop out of Arnold was to wait till he was ready to tell. I got a hint, though, when a girl appeared in the doorway; she was done up in a bikini bra and hiphuggers and she took to prancing about on the flagstones like she had to pee, squealing and waving to us.

I waved back. Arnold cut the engine and said, "As you see, dunderhead, we are not going directly to the mountains."

"Who's that?"

"That is a she whose name happens to be Nancy-baby. And don't forget the baby. To gain acceptance with this fine group"—gaining acceptance having become a big joke with us by then—"you must not call her simply Nancy. It's Nancy-baby."

Arnold had that way of talking down on you. It caused some to get their backs up but I understood it for the

12

parody it was and played back on it. "How about if I call her Honeypot?"

"No no no, dunderhead! You must leave that and other such cruddy, cornball endearments behind you now. All the propriety and dignity you can possibly muster will undoubtedly fall far short of the mark, but do, please, make the effort."

I let out a weightlifter's grunt to indicate my willingness.

"Do not get carried away, my dear man. She's to be taken for granted, like cocktails. And, come to think of it, along with cocktails, and that comes later. For the nonce, you oaf, I'm most anxious that you make a favorable impression upon the hostess who has invited . . . Well, she's invited me and I've invited you."

Since the only one in sight was Nancy-baby, I assumed, then, that she was the hostess.

"The point is, she's newmoney, sir, and so you are being given one more chance."

He'd given me many one-more-chances.

"You may be just her meat—it's unlikely but possible. So when I introduce you, I want you at your most charming, and we do know what charming is, don't we, dunderhead? That's when you show as many teeth as you can and nod your stupid head every so often, and above all don't *say* anything. Don't even *think*. Uncle Arnie will talk you up the right portfolio and *then*— Hey, are you listening to me?"

No, I wasn't. I was imagining introducing it to her with cocktails.

Now Arnold had the car trunk open and was stuffing my swim trunks into his bag. He gave me the bag to carry and we walked over the gravel driveway toward Nancy-baby, who came running to meet us halfway. She and Arnold went into a bearhug and spun around a few times.

"Arnie! Why didn't you write? You never even phoned! For a whole year!"

Which he dismissed with: "Bay-bee! You look positively scrumptious! Ah, if you only knew what joy it brings just to feast my *eyes* on you! I think you've lost a little weight."

I stood there unintroduced, just holding the bag and praying to the lovely bouncy bosomy glory of Nancy-baby's body—big, plump, wasp-waisted, surrealistically curvacious. She faced the world with a wide and friendly smile and big blue eyes that begged to please. I begged back from the sidelines and sort of itched, and finally we moved on up the flagstones toward the front door.

Then, as we went through the door, I spotted a large cluster of collegiates in the style and aspect of Arnold. They were on the far side of the room and they were wearing those colorful, casual clothes that never seem to spot or wrinkle, standing around in fashion poses, being ever so relaxed and casual—with such chin-up, straight-backed stiffness that it gives away the pose. I knew them instantly for a conglomeration of the sons and daughters of the rich and powerful. Except for a few—Nancy-baby, for instance—they were the standard: those girls I'd encountered at the swim club the past two summers with their cool, lean, tight little princessly ways, and those big, beefy boys with their roundish puffed-up asses I'd been

14

seeing in locker rooms since my early teens whenever our team met prep schools.

The whole brace of them were pretending not to notice us, for reasons which eluded me then, and they were pretending too much. There were about two dozen or more, and they were deployed into four or five chitchat groups, going about this in their own way of making announcements to each other and turning smiles on and off like neon signs. Arnold had dropped me into our society's cream before, but it had never been as homogeneous a mixture as this.

Anyhow, he broke off his inane chatter in the foyer and said, "Oh yes, Randy, this is Nancy-baby. And, dear heart, this dolt is my friend, the olympus prospect." He was always careful to say olympus instead of olympics. "Avoid him like the plague."

I did my best to send the message of my poorboy's purple-headed passion as we nodded to each other, then we all moved further into the house, and it was here that I began to come undone. There was too much to see and hear all at once. And besides trying to pick up crumbs from the conversations of the uppercrusties, I was becoming a hang-jawed gawker at the room we were entering.

It was three stories high up through the middle, with balconies jutting out every which way. There were stone arches to go under and a lighted aquarium, the biggest I've ever seen outside a zoo. It stood as high as most rooms are and was as long as a backyard swimming pool, and its colored lights bathed the whole room. But the big jolt came after a moment of blinking the bright sunshine out of my eyes

15

when I began to see these things that looked like floating islands. They were white and I became engrossed in trying to figure out what they were.

"Forty knots in a headwind," boomed some guy from the far end of the room. "Make it to Bimini in any kind of weather."

"Oh Charles," said a girl, "you're not serious."

Nancy-baby took a few steps toward the lot of them and her voice rose over the general din: "Boys upstairs, girls down. Boys upstairs, girls down." But they ignored that interesting command—ignored her completely.

She gave up and came back and stood beside Arnold, who quickly distracted her attention from the snubbing she'd just been given. I was still gawking when I became aware of another female close at hand, but I went right on trying to blink the sun out of my eyes, trying to make out what all the globs of white were.

Arnold was saying, "Randy, this is Cash."

Cash? I couldn't imagine what transaction he had in mind.

He laughed. "Randy, I want you to meet our hostess, Cash. Her *name* is Cash!"

And the girl at my side was laughing at the expression on my face.

Arnold's leer broadened as he relished springing that name on me and he babbled on: "You see, dunderhead, you are privy as the first outsider to this annual rite, and I hope you have the good grace to appreciate it. Those charming young ladies over there are erstwhile lizzies from Cash's old boarding school, and those gentlemen are, cough-cough, old comrades-in-arms from my old alma

16

mater, the brother boarding school, and we are gathered here today for the third annual release from the strains and tensions of final examinations."

"Well," said Cash, looking him over in a calculating, critical way, "we're not going to let go this time like we did last year or the year before. Bear that in mind, Arnold."

"Yes, oh yes. Of course!"

I said, "What happened last year?"

"Never mind," she snapped.

"Sweetheart," said Arnold, draping an arm around her shoulder, "meet Randy, the olympus prospect."

"Charmed," she said without the slightest indication that she was. Then she looked me up and down like a wary shopper. All three of them were looking me over this way and it had me uneasy—the clothes I wore were faded from too many launderings and under the clothes I was, after all, just a plain old scruffy poorboy, not very tall and decidedly not handsome, and I was a long way from my own turf.

Then Cash ended this with: "Make yourself at home, Randy. Any friend of Arnold's is a friend of ours."

Ours brought my attention back to Nancy-baby, who stood beaming beside the expressionless Cash. I had to force myself to accept the idea that Nancy-baby wasn't the hostess, that Cash was.

Cash, in contrast to Nancy-baby's exposed bustiness, was dressed in a sweater and skirt, and instead of the big bright-eyed smile, she had deep-set brown eyes that peered up from under her brows with a certain suspiciousness. There was something sad about her, too, like she'd just

17

heard of the death of her next of kin but was determined not to spoil anyone else's fun by allowing her real feelings to show.

They were waiting for me to react now, to do or say something, so I turned to a perpendicular lump of white just inside the door and said, "What's this? Somebody's ghost?"

It was a bedsheet, I discovered when I went to it and fingered it. I tried to locate an end so I could lift it up and peek under, for I was downright feverish by this time to know what the hell was under all these cottonpicking globs of white.

Cash's hand came to my aid, found a loose end and together we raised the sheet to behold an empty suit of knight's armor, standing there in hollow gallantry gripping a lance. She mentioned something about what country and century it was from, which I didn't listen to; I dug the change of mood put into the room by this gone individual.

Arnold and Nancy-baby stood side by side, watching— he leeringly, she smiling brightly—waiting for me to let my reaction be known.

Which, I strongly felt, I'd better keep to myself. I was sure it would not meet with approval here—worse, I feared it would reveal itself to them anyhow, in spite of my attempt to hide it.

So I tried to switch their attention by cupping an ear to hear the chatter coming to us from the other end of the room. The voice of a girl rose above the others: "Ski, ski, ski! I want to ski! You *did* bring your skis, didn't you, Harold?"

They were deciding who would go waterskiing, who

18

sailboating, who surfing, who yachting. In all my years of competitive swimming I'd never been sailboating or yachting, and I was feeling an urge to dash into their midst shouting, "Yeah, yeah, yeah! Me too!"

Instead of which, I brought my attention to the largest lump of sheet in the room. It loomed majestically in the middle of the floor, about two feet taller than I and as long as a high-priced car, and as I moved toward it, the horde of uppercrusties dispersed, like I'd given some signal or I had b.o., or something.

The boys went up the stairs in groups of two or three, and the girls went around the foot of the stairs and into a door, back there, a parting of the sexes accompanied by cheery good-byes and see-you-on-the-yacht calls. Then Arnold and Nancy-baby brushed by me and he shoved my thin nylon racing trunks into my pocket and draped the jockstrap over my shoulder, and said, "When you're finished down here, there's a room upstairs to change in."

At the foot of the stairs, he gave Nancy a parting hug, then she followed the girls and he went up the stairs after the boys.

Which left me alone with the hostess in this huge, high room. She watched as I circled this big pile of sheet, then she went deftly about the job of uncovering it.

To reveal the statue of a horse, like out of King Arthur's Court, all decked out in the paraphernalia of the tilting contest and standing on a pedestal, riderless. I stood there gazing up at this stone animal, feeling her eyes on me. I stood there thinking how absurd it was—grotesque, some sort of sick joke on the Metropolitan Museum downtown. I stood there wondering what the hell it was doing here, in

19

a house, and particularly in this house way out here. Why wasn't it in a museum? Or was this house a museum? But if it was a museum, why was everything all covered up? Anyhow, why would anybody want to turn a house into a museum?

This must have showed on my face, for I felt her growing resentment like a breeze lightly on my neck. I forced myself to say something: "And, eh, what are all these . . ." waving an arm at the other islands of white.

She began lightheartedly but her tone trailed off and ended on the black keys: "Oh, all sorts of things. Statues, knights, figurines, relics. You name it, we've got it. They're not all originals, of course. Very few originals. But, come on, I'll show you."

We redraped the horse and moved on to a British lion —on his haunches guarding a huge fireplace which hadn't been used, I guessed, for many a year. It was directly across the room from the aquarium and the colored lights from that danced in its gloomy insides like some dim memory of its last fire.

Cash gave me some tourguiding chatter about the lion, then the question that bugged me just sort of slipped out: "But what's it *for?*"

"For! He's not *for* anything."

"Well, eh, I mean, what's it *doing* here?"

"He's not doing anything. He's simply here."

"Oh. Well, eh, like why?"

She was agitated; my questions were putting her on the defensive so I decided to pursue this role, hostess-agitator. It seemed the best way I could think of to break the ice. Besides, her defensiveness eased my awkwardness.

20

"Must it have a reason?" she snapped. "It's been here all along. It's been here since we bought the place. It's one of the oldest pieces here."

I rolled my eyes meaningfully away, scanning the other globs and piles of sheet. Truly, I felt, it was incredible that anyone would want to have all these things in a house, to just put them down here and cover them up. For what?

"Your family," I tried, "own this place?"

"Of course."

"And, eh, all this . . ."

"Yes."

"Well, eh, why do you cover everything up?"

It seemed a reasonable question to me—just as it seemed unreasonable to her. "To protect them," she said, as if to a retarded child. "To keep the dust off them." And now her eyes were wide.

"Oh," I said as snidely as I could, "I see. You collect all this junk and you cover it up."

And that really brought her on.

"Junk!"

"Sorry," I taunted. "What is it?"

"There are many, many items in this house, but none of it is junk!"

She had such sharply proper enunciation that I was tempted to call her on switching from the plural, "items," to the singular, "it." Instead, I leaned back against the stairway banister to enjoy her anger. Which, I reasoned, was to be valued second only to her ardor, as opposed to her indifference. So I leaned and listened as she chewed words at me.

21

"As I *told* you, we have very *few* originals, *and,* I'm afraid, *no* masterpieces, as *such*. But I'm *sure* that if you were *really int*erested you'd find we *do* have an ex*cep*tionally well-*bal*anced collection."

About which I couldn't have cared less—it was the intensity of her concern that delighted me.

"And," she added, "there are many, many *very* fine copies here. Made by *real* craftsmen. *From* the originals!"

"Wayll," I said in my most downhome country drawl, rubbing my head as if at a crossword puzzle in Swahili, "if you like having them, why d'ye cover them up?"

"To pro*tect* them, I *told* you!" And with this, my face got a fine, damp shower from her hot breath.

I hauled out a handkerchief with Arnold's monogram on it and made a big to-do of wiping my face. Then I sighed to quietly register my own exasperation, and led us on to the next undraping—another hollow suit of armor, this one clutching a sword and standing like a bombed-out guardian of the bottom of the stairs.

I quickly covered it back up again. "Pretty big house you have here."

"Huge."

"Like a hotel."

"Bigger than most hotels."

"And you *live* here—"

"No! Of course not!"

"What? It just sits here empty? I mean, full. Full of . . . all this. Doesn't anybody live here?"

"Just the caretakers and a cat."

"Like, eh, what could be more sensible than that? Like, why should anybody live here—right?"

22

Which brought back a cold glare. She was fed up trying to show me around, so I said, "Mind if I look around?"

"There's really nothing to *see*. *Is* there?"

"Well . . . I mean, just roam around and see all this nothing."

Silence.

"Do you mind?"

"I suppose not. As long as you *are* careful."

"Thank you kindly."

"But don't you *dare* . . ." she said with tremors, *"break* anything."

Then she turned and made a hasty exit around the foot of the stairs, saying caustically, "Any friend of Arnold's is a friend of ours."

I took her tone as applause for my performance, all that venom she put into it. I was tempted to crow a loud laugh as I watched her moving away, her back stiff, shoulders squared. I didn't know how long this party would last, but having rattled the hostess, I was off to a rolling start. With good luck and the proper timing, I'd come away a winner—so I thought.

3

IN THOSE DAYS I was trying to live my life the way I swam my best races. I was a skilled practitioner of what we used to call the rolling start—I didn't start after the gun went off, I was going *when* the gun went off. That is, I didn't rely on my reflexes, which were quick enough—I timed the starter, tried to get with just how long it took him under what circumstances, from the time he said, "Take your marks," to when he fired his blank so that I'd be reacting when he pulled the trigger instead of reacting and winding up to get a-goin' after the shot. And in my specialty, the 200-yard butterfly, I liked to go all out the first lap, then coast and save my stuff for the final lap, moving out at the end with everything I had. I was a comer-from-behind, not an all-out giver to the race the whole way.

It paid off, in swimming. My skill at the rolling start got me off ahead in most races and I'd hit that first turn out in front, giving the competition that early first worry of having to catch me. Then I'd fox them and loaf. If I was up against someone with about the same best time as my own, I'd let him pass me early in the second lap, then let him pull me along like a psychological burden. I'd hang on his heels, keeping an eye on him underwater

24

and let him set the pace, giving him his second worry —that maybe he was putting out too much too soon. I'd try to prove his worst fears the truth by picking up the pace coming into the last turn, then pouring it on for all I was worth coming down that last lap. Because to get passed at this point, that's what really sucks the life right out of you. And in those big last laps, to help the flow of my adrenalin, I'd chant in time to my strokes as I exhaled into the water, "Give *up*, you bastard, give *up!* Give *up*, you bastard, give *up!*" And I'd keep a hard eye on him underwater—first his feet, then his torso, until I'd swallowed him and was ahead and feeling like the last ounce of strength he'd had for the race had just gone over to me and I was adding it to my own now, right up to that last lunging stroke that drove me to the touch.

And I wanted to live my life that way—swallow up many a competitor coming out of the last turn and down the homestretch, suck the life out of him just when he thought he had a big win and come lunging home to steal the goodies he thought he had. This was the sort of outlook I was bringing to that party, and to that first exchange with Cash. And I felt that if I could keep her off balance and agitated, I'd have my way with her, with the lot of them. I'd get off to a rolling start, then hang back and take the pack of them at the party's final turn—any party's final turn. And of course that outlook—in this situation—was self-defeating, but I didn't want to know that then.

Anyhow, I was setting out on my tour of the house now and meeting the competition. They were coming down as I was going up the main stairway. They'd changed into bathingsuits—or, to be more precise, beach attire. They looked like colorful paper cutouts from the men's fashion pages. A few carried surfboards so bright and shiny, so brand spanking new they made me vaguely hungry.

The first one I met said, with his eyes on something behind me, "Hello, there," and passed by.

The next was a bit friendlier and said, just a touch gay, "Hi."

Then came a clutch of about five or six, out of whose midst stepped a tough-featured, athletic-looking butch. "Hello there, I don't believe we've met." There were introductions all around in their style of overripe friendliness, their ploy to put off an outsider without seeming to. It was like stopping for gas in a ghost town. Except for the handshakes—they came at me all toting ready right hands with a quick, firm grip, something like gunslingers out of old Westerns.

They went on down the stairs then, and converged with girls coming out of the room down there. They didn't pair off, but went as one long strung-out troop through the sliding glass doors, all chattering about waterskis, sailboats, yachts and the condition of the surf.

Near the top of the stairs I met another covey of boys and there was another round of introductions. Then all but one of them went on down the stairs; the one that lingered was staring at me, just standing there staring.

"You're Arnold's friend, aren't you?"

"Yes."

"Well, would you mind if I ask you a personal question?"

I'd seen that sheepishly intent look in other eyes, heard that conspiratorial tone before.

"No, I don't mind. What's the question?"

"Are—eh, eh. Now don't get angry, I'm not trying to insult you or anything. I mean we're all broadminded here, you know."

"Sure."

"But what I want to know is, are you—eh—a bisexual too?"

"Oh no," I said quickly, "I'm a five-sexual."

"A what?"

"Five-sexual. Straight, bi, homo, an occasional lizzie and an animal or two," I half-lied.

"Animals!" he said, profoundly horrified.

"You ever tried any?"

"Oh God!"

And with that, he made his way rapidly down the steps and disappeared out the door—to spread the word, I was sure.

Then, almost immediately, another was at me, walking toward me with his head lowered like a monk contemplating. He halted in front of me, scanned me, my clothes, from head to toe, and he said, "You're not one of us."

"No."

"And neither am I," he added without even blinking, and went past me, down the steps.

You're not one of us and neither am I! Wow, I thought, how very American.

By this time I was on the second-floor landing and was stopping to undrape the white lump that perched at the top of the banister. It was a Roman bust, a solemn mug with curly hair; he looked a little like a prize-fight champion. I tweaked his nose—he had the sort of face that brought that out of me.

On the wall nearby I found a rack of ancient lances hanging like pool cues in a tall glass case. Down the hall a short way, I found a glass-encased collection of primitive pistols, and near that a brotherly collection of ancient rifles. I'd de-sheeted all three of these glass cases so I took time out to pull their sheets neatly back over them before I pressed on into the bowels of the house.

I went along opening doors into bedrooms and peeking in. It was all one mass of white sheet at first glance, with only patches of bare hardwood floor, patches of bare walls—otherwise these rooms were practically flooded by sheet.

In the first room I hit, there was a bed in an alcove, and near that was a wax figure, a young woman wearing nightclothes from out of fourteenth-century England, I would guess. In another, the bed was canopy-topped and there was, under a sea of sheet-covered tables, much bric-a-brac and period pieces of furniture that matched the bed.

Each room, I discovered, was from a certain time and place, and the things in it had been selected to reflect that time and place, and everything—in all the rooms and in the hallways and on the balconies—was under masses and lumps and piles of sheet, room after room, hallway after hallway.

Along one long hallway there was a row of hip-high piles of sheet like a mountain range with steep peaks. Which, uncovered, turned out to be tables with displays of little figurines. Each table had a scene—a blacksmith shop, women at spinning wheels, grain harvesters and grain millers—with six- or eight-inch-tall people frozen in the various postures of doing their business.

Everything I encountered in the house was out of the bygones of Europe, back through Rome to the Greeks. It was a house crammed full of the relics of those old dogmas, the cultural leavings of Western European man. As, I suppose, aren't we all.

And everything I excavated from sheet was loaded with commentary. Some seemed to whisper or hint of sad endings, of busy lives and hard work done till death; others seemed to be shouting conflicting rumors on the secrets of the fleshy joys; still others, boasting of courage and conquests.

At the end of one third-floor balcony there was a sword-swinging Roman—helmet, shin-guards, the works—and he was facing a pile at the other end of the balcony which turned out to be covering a piping Pan with little horns growing out of his head. I de-sheeted them both and stood back, looking from one to the other; facing each other this way they seemed to be having some sort of disagreement. The expressions they wore filled the silence, my imagination heard shouts from them both, and I stayed with them a long time—until the dust I'd stirred up flinging their sheets around caused me to sneeze.

I eventually found that it was a complicated and pretentious old place, that house, with two wings—north and south—with balconies out over the main room from the second and third floors, outside balconies, and hallways that seemed to lead every which way. With all the windows boarded up, I kept finding myself deep in the thick silence of some long hall, wondering if I'd been here before, or where this one might lead, suspecting I was going in circles. Somehow, in my wanderings, I made it from the north wing to the south, for I found myself on a balcony right above the aquarium and across the main room from the stairway I'd gone up to begin with. None of the doors I tried were locked, none of the displays barred to inspection, so I kept going—through one room onto an outside balcony overlooking the grounds in front of the house, up this stairway and that, into at least a dozen rooms. I ended up, finally, on the roof by way of a ladder up to a trapdoor that opened into a little lookout nest up there.

And, sure enough, this place was, for a certain, out in nowhere. As far as I could see in any direction there was nothing—no houses, no sign of human life. The house had been put down here in surroundings so lonely they seemed cosmic. The only sign of humanity anywhere was right down below me—on the patio, on the beach in front of it and in the ocean just off the beach. All else was a vast expanse of desolation, of sea and sky, sand and greenery.

For a long time I was spellbound by the very impersonal mood of this surrounding vastness, soaking it up like it was some nearly silenced music coming to me in the wind. Then I turned my attention to what was going on with—as I'll damn well keep on calling them—the sons and daughters of the rich and powerful.

They were playing. In a gracefully austere way, and rather solemnly, it seemed to me from up here, they had things and were playing with them. It looked like a busy construction site, complete with buzz, sputter and putt-putt.

Someone had brought an outboard and it was zooming around in the ocean on the swells just past the breakers, toting waterskiers who took turns going for rides. There was one of those small sailboats you have to lean over the side of to keep it from tipping, and a couple was putting it through its paces while the outboard went buzzing around making wakes that threatened to topple the sailboat. Further out, a yacht was being put to some sort of maneuverability test, and on the beach there was a coeducational game of touch football being played with a big beachball, girls against the boys. All of them were playing with something except one pair of them, the Lovers, and they were lying on a blanket locked in a busy embrace, playing with each other.

In the shallows, with the foamy surf hitting them in the thighs, stood three girls having a little confab. This was broken up when three boys dashed down the beach, into the shallows, and went splashing after the girls. Each caught himself a girl and they messed around awhile, then they regrouped, and the girls climbed onto the shoulders of the boys and a game of queen-dethronement got underway. Right off, two of the girls ganged up on the third and were both trying to knock her off, and it was about now that I realized who this third girl was: Nancy-baby. She was giving her attackers a worthy defense and it looked for a time like she'd end up besting the both of them.

Then, presently, the style of their tussling changed. It became something closer to what you'd expect to find in a low dive in the wee hours of a payday night. One girl had herself a handful of Nancy's hair and was tugging away for all she was worth and the other was flailing her arms like a windmill, raining blows on Nancy's back and shoulders, arms and face. Nancy finally went down, toppled by the hair-puller and dragging the flailer down with her. The puller then slid off the shoulders of her boy and the three girls stood in the water arguing. That was broken up when one of the boys went back to the beach, picked up a couple of surfboards and carried them out. Now, all but Nancy took to surfing, taking turns paddling out and coasting in. Nancy turned and walked through the water to the beach and stood there watching the others, rubbing her upper arm. She had her weight shifted to one leg, one hip out with the hand of the injured arm resting on it. Then one of the girls, the hair-puller, while she waited her next turn on the board, put on an imitation of Nancy's stance. At this, Nancy headed for the house, bent forward, taking long strides, lumbering up through the sand.

That sent me out of my lookout, scrambling through the house, hunting for a way down. I felt a sudden something like kinship for Nancy-baby, like she was a playmate from out of my childhood and I hadn't seen her since we rolled in the clover in the summer of our eighth year and it was only now, when I saw her dumped by them, that I recognized her.

4

IT TOOK ME A WHILE to work myself out of the dark labyrinthine bowels of the house. When I got to the main room, no one was there, but from the other side of the aquarium I heard voices, Arnold's among them. I went around and found a kitchen-dining area with a bar at the far end. Arnold was playing cock of the walk, supervising three girls in the making of a large bowl of martinis, aided in this task by Cash. A matronly brown-skinned woman was in the kitchen, piling food on trays.

I went out to the patio through the sliding glass doors, into the glare of the sun's reflection on the bright tiles, squinting for Nancy-baby. She was sitting on the steps leading down from the patio to the beach, and she was looking like the kid nobody wants to play with. Just sitting there staring out at the goings-on, the waterskiing and buzzing boats, and she was rubbing her left arm.

Which, I found when I reached her, had a nasty scratch on it. I stood by looking her over for a time, then she became aware of my nearness and turned and looked up at me very seriously. Immediately she wiped off that expression and flashed me her big warm grin and sparkling blue eyes, and said, "Hi."

"Hi, what happened to your arm?"

33

"Oh we were messing around down there and Karen scratched me."

But she didn't seem put out about it; her sparkle and smile remained. She was on the top step, sprawled in a careless way, scrunched down on the tail of her backbone with her weight on the bare skin just above the low waist of her bikini. She seemed completely relaxed and un-concerned—her legs stretched out, dark brown hair hanging down wet and stringy. Her limbs were solidly plump, not fat plump, and she sort of radiated good health, like a girl from a dairy farm come to the big city to get photo-graphed for a milk advertisement. She'd never make it anywhere near any Miss America-type contest—her smile was too toothy for that, her nose too broad, her body too classically proportioned, and the expression on her face declared that here was a person with vulnerable sensitivities, virgin goodnaturedness.

I made a big thing out of inspecting the scratch, then I wondered out loud if it shouldn't have a dab of iodine, or something, and if we could find such a thing as iodine somewhere in the many-celled insides of the house. She in-sisted it didn't need medicine, that it just stung a little from the saltwater, but she seemed so bright-eyed pleased by my attentions that I persisted. And the fingernails of Karen had, after all, drawn blood. I said, "Come on, let's try to find something." And she came with me into the house.

I'd encountered some bathrooms in my travels, so I led her up the main stairway and down the hall, hunting for one I dimly recalled being near the top of the main stairway.

She was still wearing her big grin, as if she was delighted

34

by my solicitous attentions. It wasn't what I thought of as the standard princess-type smile, the off-and-on neon sign; it seemed like the true barometer of her real feelings.

"You go to that boarding school with Cash?"

"Uh huh. And I'm her roommate at the university too."

"Hmm. You make the party last year?"

"Sure, and the year before that."

"Tell me something—how long do these shindigs last?"

"All night, usually."

"Yeah? Wow. Ah, here's that bathroom. Come on."

And inside it, as I rummaged through an incongruously ordinary cabinet above an ordinary sink, I said, "What happens at these parties? Like what's the action? Do they swing?"

She didn't reply. And when I glanced at her, the smile had disappeared, the blue eyes were far away, staring off into space. Her face had dropped to a downward dejection.

"Hey, what's the trouble? Did I say something?"

She pinched her eyes tight shut and her lips trembled, and she seemed on the verge of tears. I got an urge to put my arms around her and comfort her with a hug, so I did. Then she sort of leaned against me and I automatically went to soothing and stroking her back, and the next thing I knew she had her face against my shoulder—she was crying quietly, with a steady lurching and bumping against me. I cradled her as best I could and began rocking her a little, like you do a baby, and I kept asking, "Hey, what's wrong, what's the trouble?" But she just went on crying softly, tears rolling down her cheeks onto my shirt.

At the time I felt sure—though I didn't mention it—

35

that the treatment she'd gotten during the game of queen-dethronement had hurt her enough so that here, away from them, she had come off that broad smile that had seemed so real, and she was giving in to the real hurt she was feeling.

Meanwhile, I was having mixed emotions—I was feeling for her, knowing in myself the hurt she must be feeling—but at the same time I was unable to keep myself from being aroused by all that glowingly healthy naked flesh pressed against me. It wasn't long before we had between us, bumped and rubbed by her lurching and the cuddling and rocking, a firm indication of this, and she couldn't help knowing it.

Then the whole affair suddenly took on a brand-new mood: she adjusted her rocking movements to it, this emissary of her effect on me; she half-turned and now we were front to front and I could feel her hips thrusting forward, and when I let my hand go to her barely covered plump rump, I felt her buttocks tightening and relaxing, tightening and relaxing. Then she lifted her face from my shoulder and was breathing hard past my ear. "Go ahead!" she whispered. "Go ahead, I don't care. Get it over with! I just don't care any more."

I wasn't at all clear about how we'd gone from friend-liness to tearfulness to this. I wasn't even clear about what this now was. Clearly, though, this was not the time to try and figure it out—I was too much in favor of it to question it—and since I'd spotted a bottle of medicine, and also because I needed a moment to collect my wits, I sent one hand up to bring it down and unscrew the top and, keeping the other arm tightly around her, I went to work dabbing the scratch.

And when the medicine touched her scratch, she hissed in air and rubbed and rolled herself against me. Now she had her arms around me and was letting out little moans. She was carrying on over the medicine, I tried to suppose—till she hooked one leg around the back of mine and I was being hugged so well I knew it was more, a whole lot more. I kept dabbing and thanking fate for answering my prayers so quickly, and she kept hissing and hugging, and everything was surprisingly close to real fine—except, where in this sheet-covered honeycomb of rooms could we go?

The third floor, I decided, and with that I dropped the dabber to the floor and set the medicine bottle on the sink, and said, "Come on, let's go." We untangled and went out to the hall and headed for the main stairway; we were holding hands and I was feeling elated with delightful expectation. Till we were going past the top of the main stairway and a high-pitched sharp angry female voice hit us: *"Nancy!"*

She flinched like a gun had gone off near her ear.

Cash stood at the bottom of the stairs, hands on hips, scowling up at us like a bossy mama. She stomped her foot and said, *"Oh! Honestly!"*

Which seemed strangely appropriate to me. But not to Nancy. She bolted away, frightened; she spun around and looked horrified down at Cash, and she stood there tugging at her low-hanging bikini pants and adjusting her bra like she'd been caught in the nude by the cops.

37

Cash said, with her teeth clenched and her lips compressed, "Must this *always* happen?"

There was a small, pathetic sound out of Nancy, like a pup that's just wet on the living-room rug and expects a slap.

"Year after year after year!" yelled Cash, stomping her foot three times.

"Oh no! I'm *sorry*!" came the peep from the pup.

"You always regret it, oh you always regret!"

"I know."

"But you said, *not* this time. You promised me it wouldn't happen this time. Didn't you?"

"Yes."

"Well . . . ? *What* are you doing?"

"I had a little scratch, I didn't want to—"

"But you *were,* you *were,* you were going *some*place, weren't you?"

"He—"

"*Will* you promise me something?"

"Yes."

"Don't! Not this time."

"Oh yes, I promise."

"And will you *keep* that promise now?"

"Yes."

"Besides! Who is that . . . that *thing* you're with?"

"He's—he's a friend of Arnold's. Isn't he?"

They both looked at me, Nancy with wide-eyed wonder and Cash with wide-eyed outrage.

"Well," said Cash in a most poisonous tone, "he *looks* harmless enough." Then, switching to a put-on warmth: "But please, honey, why should we let him embarrass us?"

38

"Oh I won't. I promise."

And by this time, Nancy was on her way down the stairs. Cash took her by the arm and led her away toward the girls room, and then, from the other side of the aquarium, stepped Arnold. He strolled coolly into the main room leering broadly and he slumped back to lean against the jamb of an opened door; he let out a short, loud laugh and said, "Foiled!"

"So it damn well seems," I said.

"And it's a good thing you were, dunderhead. You'd have upset everything."

"How?"

"Never mind that now. Come on down here, you dunce, and have a drink with me. And a talk, oaf, because I have a plan. An overall masterplan has suggested itself to my fertile mind, and I feel compelled to share it with you, you undeserving clod. Otherwise, you're liable to wreck the party."

"How?" But he was gone—outside onto the patio. I went down the stairs two at a time and followed him out.

5

A LONG WOODEN TABLE had been moved out to the patio and on it was a big cutglass punchbowl filled to the brim with martini. The bowl was attended by a cluster of longstemmed glasses, very fancy and elegant, with a fragile pride in the style of most of the guests—and the clear liquid and glasswear all dazzled in the bright sun, attracting the eye like a shrine to some unnamed religious sect.

I rejoined Arnold at it and we ladled ourselves out drinks with a silver dipper. Then, holding our longstemmed glassfuls of martini reverently before us, we went like acolytes to a place on the bench that was built against a wall that went around the patio. It was one long flowerbox, this wall, with green shrubs and bright blooms all waving and bobbing in the breezes.

Arnold was being meaningfully silent for the moment, the way he usually got when he was about to come up with one of his masterplans, so I was looking at the big eye-catcher out here—a fountain, a stone pond rimmed by a circle of statues. And I was just getting tuned in on this spectacle when the door to the girls' room slid open and Cash stepped out, carrying a cat. She had it cradled in one arm and was stroking its back and she was making

40

a beeline for us. She walked up with her eye sharp on me and she said, "Arnold, may I have a word with you?"

"Of course," said Arnold.

And she still had her eye sharp on me. "Alone," she said.

"All right," said Arnold, and he parked his glass and got up, and it was right here that brother cat pulled his thing—he hopped out of her arms and down to me, and stood on my thigh looking seriously up at me.

"But baby," I said, "this is so sudden." And was about to pet him when she snatched him back by the nape of his neck and held him up to her ear, like listening to him purr.

"Come, come, Diogenes," she said to him, "don't be that way. We're just having a little party."

She listened to him some more and said, "I *know* you don't like it, but you're not the *only* one to be considered. Oh. This is Arnold's friend, I forget his name." With emphasis on forget. "I leave you with him." And dropped him back onto my thigh.

Then she turned and, with Arnold following in his posture of exaggerated humility, marched back into the girls' room. I fondled the cat awhile and we looked each other over pretty good. He was a healthy, stealthy critter of a technicolored hue with a lot of orange in his fur and some streaks of white, so we kind of recognized each other as kindred mongrel spirits. I gave him a serious petting and he gave me some serious purring, then he shoved off and went walking flowingly over the sun-sparkled terrazzo deck of the patio, pausing once to glance back as if he just had an afterthought he wished to convey. I was involved in

41

trying to read him, countryboy that I am, when Cash stuck her head back out of the girls' room and hollered over at me. "Say," she said, like it was an uppercrust vulgarization of "Hey." "Say, you might want to survey the statues out here. Add them to your tour."

I nodded, and she said, "They're my father's pride and joy." Very seriously, like maybe warning me that I'd damn well better value them. "They were done from the Greek originals."

I nodded again and she disappeared into the room. She's some funny chick, I said to myself. Maybe she thinks putting me next to these statues will turn me off Nancy-baby. But what's it to her, anyhow? What's she care what Nancy and I do? Yeah, she's some funny chick. I wonder what she wants. Maybe she's getting up a threesome in there with Nancy and Arnold. Like maybe she wants to take care of Nancy herself. Or maybe she wants to supervise while Arnold does.

But there seem to be no maybes about what I could do about it—I can go stare at statues. So I did. Walked over to this fountain in the middle of this round stone pond. The rim of it came about up to my shin, and on this rim was this circle of stone figures that were supposed to be Greek. In the middle of the pond was a definitely un-Greek cherub who spouted water from his mouth. A fine sturdy little specimen with chubby limbs, a cute little uncircumcised cock and a round tight sack of testicles. He'd been caught and stoned in the act of leaping and shouting some joyous news and I felt a bit sorry for him —the way they'd given him plumbing and water to squirt quashed the spirit of his message.

Around the rim of the fountain, males alternated with females all facing in the same direction—toward the center of the patio. They all seemed very docile, too, like they'd been arriving for a friendly orgy when they got caught and petrified. They were all naked and had fine physiques —except for one thing. It seemed to me that whoever made them had insulted them, because the arms, legs, torsos and faces were formed with great care for definition, and you could see sinews in the arms of the boys, even indentations in the bottoms of their noses for nostrils. But they'd been cheated in their sex organs: the girls had barely any nipples at all and the cocks and balls of the boys lacked anything close to the fine definition of their faces, torsos, arms and legs. Each toe on every foot was definitely a toe, right down to the toenail, but the cocks and balls were practically malformed lumps, like the models had posed in jockstraps. Only the little cherub's sex had good definition—the youths were shortchanged.

Her father's pride and joy, eh. Must be very patriotic, her father—one of those sadistic, fascist-type patriots. Probably devotes half his time trying to figure how to spend his money without spreading the joy. Imagine some old dollar-glutted duff out on the town, meets some chick he's wild about. Right away he's got that hang-up of his kind: should he cut her in or pay her off?

But not so with these phonied-up Greek youths, for he *owns* them. Has them set up this certain way, like all presenting themselves to his dreamlife for whatever he feels inclined to do-dream with them. The old goat, they're probably his favorite love-objects. I can see him now, sitting out here of a breezy summer evening, sipping a cocktail

43

and puffing a fat cigar, masturbating mentally on all these fine stone youths, all presenting themselves stripped for action and about to step toward him slavishly offering their bowdlerized selves, and never giving him his old worry: should he cut them in or pay them off?

But no doubt what these figures were putting into my head about her father—as I hark back on it here—tells you more about me. Anyhow, I was glad I could give them a good looking over without Cash around to interrupt my imaginings, to pelt me with the garbage of her version of the facts.

And just as I was feeling glad about this, here she was at my side. Which gave me a jolt; I didn't know how long she'd been hovering by, and it was a little like being caught with the goods. She was looking at me like she was sure I'd be snickering about the nudity and she was all set to let fly a lecture on "culture."

"Well?" she said, "What do you think?"

A fast pointblank question I was slow to answer, all things considered.

"Gee," I tried, "I bet they cost a lot of money."

"Oh, yes! Quite a bit! Daddy hired the sculptor himself and sent him to Europe. But, as you can see, it was worth it. They're priceless."

I belched. And loudly. It just slipped out and wasn't intended as a comment, though it did make a good one. Too good. She sucked in a breath and took off. Again I'd insulted her.

So I left the circle of Greeks and went back to the bench. Cash was busy supervising in the kitchen now; Arnold and Nancy-baby were still absent from my sight.

44

A recordplayer had been brought out and put on the table about a yard from the bowl of clear liquid and now a group of them were sorting through stacks of records and chattering about who was going to put what record on. There was one tall fellow with a shock of dark hair falling down to his eyebrows, who looked very serious and intense, standing by holding some records, waiting. Then, while the others went on chattering, he went to the record-player and put one on; soon the strident strains of a rather militant classic boomed out. I sat there thinking how aptly pompous it was, how it gave musical voice to the spiritual ancestors of these elegants, those bygone colonists, and was thus soothing and pampering my prejudice when I noticed that this selection had not met with unanimous approval. After a conference of the dissident at the far end of the table, a girl stepped forth, lifted the needle and replaced the classic with another.

Suddenly there burst forth a hoedown fiddle and a twanging straight out of Nashville and a group of them now clustered around to listen closely with their heads lowered, their bodies motionless, their faces studious— paying attention like attention was dues money. They paid such strict and serious attention it bordered on reverence, and it surely would have befuddled any Grand Ole Opry star to see it.

This went on for half a side of a longplay. Then, having paid their dues to the more rambunctious wailings of the nation's lowlier folk, they seemed satisfied and the country music was replaced by the loud, demanding guitars and drums of a current jukebox hit.

Which moved one daughter of the rich and powerful

45

into a solo dance. Well, no, it didn't really move her—she moved herself. She wore tight white shorts and a nipple-pink blouse; she was ash blond and standard—I mean she'd fit right into one of those old class-B-movie chorus lines. As for her dancing, it came on very limp in spirit and competent of motion, like she'd been thoroughly trained. I felt embarrassed for her.

And depressed, myself, because up till about a year ago I'd been an enthusiastic dancer, quick to be moved by most any rhythm. But during the past year or so, this quick responsiveness had left me, gone. I don't know why. It was very mysterious, but I'd suddenly discovered one night that instead of the music moving me, I was moving myself, trying to get with it and never quite making it, never quite reaching that state where the music had me and was dancing me, and since then I'd had to dance myself, like this girl doing the solo now.

Still, I told myself as I sat there sipping martini and watching her, there was one distinct difference. She'd never known what it is to be moved by this music, and I had. Because this style of music—the best of it—has the rumble of some still unformed, unborn revolution in it, and hints of defiance against the rich and powerful which this daughter of them just naturally couldn't feel. She couldn't feel it, and for her to even try was—to my poorboy's way of seeing it—like trying to contract schizophrenia.

From the dancer, then, my eye roamed to the old man, the caretaker. He was off to my right not far from where the planter wall ended and the wall to the girls room began, and he was trimming the shrubs that grew out of the planter. He had his back to everyone and was

46

snip-snipping away at his hedges, oblivious to all sights and sounds around him—a large, brawny man about the shade of a chestnut with a crop of snow-white hair, a white billygoat goatee and a beer belly that hung out over his belt. His face was expressionless, a blank front just as carefully practiced as the put-on chin-up on-and-off neon smiling and grimacing being flashed by those behind him. He reminded me of my grandfather—his build and crop of short white hair, everything but his color—and I almost expected him to wheel around any second and roar out some old cornball country commentary on the scene, like: "Empty wagon does a heap of rattlin', but a full wagon rolls right along real smooth and quiet." Like my ole gran'-pappy used to do when he thought us younguns were making too much noise, trying too frantically to impress each other.

Then from the girls' room stepped Nancy-baby. She blinked in the bright sun and looked a little sheepish. I waved her over but she hesitated, like she thought she'd better not come—but she did, she came over and sat down beside me.

6

"MARTINI?"

"Okay," she said, but the smile and bright sparkle were missing. She was being guarded, like she wasn't sure she should have anything to do with me, but she was damned sure she wasn't going to get tight with me again.

Anyhow, I parked my martini on the bench and dutifully fetched her one, then sat down close beside her. She held the glass up and stared into it for a time, like her mind was somewhere else, then she took a sip and made a wry face. I pretended not to notice, put my attention on the caretaker's wife, the plump, matronly woman looking rigidly stern and keeping her eyes hard on her work. She came out carrying a big platter of lunchmeats and cheeses and put them down on the table. Cash followed carrying paper plates, then the two of them went back for more—with Cash pausing before disappearing into the house to glance over at Nancy and me and do a slight doubletake.

Surely she couldn't object to us just sitting here—partaking sippingly of the clear liquid of the general faith—could she?

The situation befuddled me. And stifled both of us—we weren't having anything to say to each other now, Nancy and I. She was tense, withdrawn.

48

Soon lunch was ready and the word had spread and the main herd from the sea and beach were coming to the patio and lining up in their wet bathingsuits by the table to get their paper plates and fill them with the sandwich makings, carry them off and gather in small groups to eat. Cash and the caretaker's wife were on the other side of the long table, dishing up salad and things, and Cash was still keeping a wary eye on Nancy and me. And Nancy, as if she were getting silent orders from Cash, moved an inch or two away from me.

"Why does she keep checking on us?" I said.

"Who?" said Nancy, but she was a bad actress.

"She keeps staring at us. Does she think we're plotting against her?"

She laughed a strained, nervous little giggle. "Gee . . . it's, well, I don't know—I mean it's the way she *is.*"

"What way is that?"

She thought hard for a moment. "She wants everybody to stay out of the house—she promised her father."

"Is *that* it?"

"Sure. Don't you believe me?"

"Eh, oh sure!"

"Hey, I'm hungry! And I don't want to drink too much. I'm getting something to eat."

She'd parked her glass on the bench and was going to the end of the line before I reacted. "Me too!" And went after her. I got in line behind her and just inside the main room I spotted Arnold, standing there watching us. When our eyes met he shook his head, wiped his brow and held up an arm in a motion that said, Now what!

I wasn't sure what. I mean I knew he'd wanted to pair

49

me off with Cash, but that hadn't worked. Anyway, what could *I* do for Cash? It was *her* party, in *her* house, and among *her* guests I had nothing going for me, no standing whatsoever. For I couldn't help supposing that, the way most of them saw things, I wasn't even up to being the bottom of their pecking order. I was *the* outsider; the only one I could see myself getting paired off with here was Nancy-baby. I figured we had something in common, Nancy and I; I figured we two were made of better stuff than the rest of them. And, for a certain, we were each, in our own way, being excluded by them.

So what the hell; *their* exclusiveness isn't *my* hang-up, I told myself, and I ignored Arnold's signal. I was standing in line behind Nancy's behind; the sun was warm and caressing and the martini was sunning me from the inside too. So I turned my mind to worthier concerns, letting my eye roam down her back to her bikinied bottom and pray about how fine those lovely hips bloomed out from that small waist, and how ripe and luscious and tantalizing were the twin globes of her bounteous butt. I even got to singing a silent sort of hymn to the glorious paradise I felt would surely be my soul's reward later on, when this party began to swing and I'd come through strong and get my hands on those luscious twin globes again, and this time, by God, I'd petition her pearly gate, gain my soul's reward, and be damned if I'd let anybody interrupt it.

It was right about now that somebody behind me bumped into me and sent me forward to bump into the object of my worship, and it was a bump which—even after all the polite excuse me's had been tendered—a bump which jolted me so much it caused my conviction to swell. And it swelled with such true fervor that it shortly seemed cloth-rippingly ready to declare its faith in no uncertain terms—it was virtually howling inside my pants, howling for the release of salvation, for a chance to make it into heaven. In fact, its faith was so fervent by now that it was signifying.

I was making an effort to conceal the significance of my truth when I noticed—when I *felt* the hot lights of another truth—Cash's. She was glaring at the two of us as we stood there a table's width away, burning the left side of my face with some kind of wide-eyed, panic-stricken hate. I made a quick glance her way and pulled away even quicker, for the eyes that met mine were scalding.

Well, I didn't understand it, this redhot concern of Cash's, but I had it to cope with anyhow, somehow, so I resorted to my most downhome countrified. The truth will out, I said to myself, and moved up snugly against Nancy's pretty ass, put my hands on her warm, bare hips and kissed her lightly on the neck. She ignored the kiss and she picked my hands off her hips, slowly, gently. And now Cash was staring fireballs and pitchforks, even leaning forward and peering down at the significance of the truth between Nancy and me, that firm conviction of flesh and blood. And hers—whatever prickishness Cash was coming on with—was between us just as big and hard, and she kept it there all during the dishing up of food onto our paper plates and even when we left to go parading—which is about what it was—when we went across the patio carrying our lunch with the eyes of the others upon us.

They were, as they'd call it, too well-bred to stare square at the state of my conviction. Instead, they were sneaking well-bred peeks, but these peeks were as thunderously loud as a bullfight crowd's *Ole!*

As we reached the steps to the beach and were settling ourselves there to eat, Arnold appeared wearing a look of pain. He leaned down and stage-whispered near my ear, "If self-control was intelligence, dunderhead, you'd be lower than a moron."

"Well . . . it's not," was all I could think to say back.

He shook his head and let out a long *"Wheeew!"* Then he sat down with us. Or, rather, he sat down between us, for I had gone to the third step down to get away from all those sneaky glances, and Nancy-baby had perched on the top step. Arnold put himself on the second step and let us know, by the way he shouldered in, that he was there to separate us.

And shortly thereafter, Cash joined us, making it a cumbersome foursome fraught with frictions I still didn't comprehend. I mean why in the hell they were both so frantic to split us up I didn't even care to know.

But I felt obliged to ask and was about to put the question to them directly, loud and clear, when the two of them got into an interesting little exchange. No sooner had Cash settled herself on the next step down from mine than Arnold came on her with: "May I congratulate you, my dear hostess, for again bringing together such a stimulating and potentially exciting group."

"It's the same group," said Cash.

"Ah, but a year older. It's developed, grown, matured, evolved. This year the possibilities are far more varied."

"I find even your humor depraved," spat Cash.

52

Arnold ignored her and went on: "As I gaze about at these happy faces and hear the wee tinkle of their delighted voices—our erstwhile brothers and sisters, so to speak— now in such lively and civilized banter, I can only but wonder—"

"Oh be quiet and eat."

"Ah ha!" said Arnold. "Who's that?" He was craning his neck to look past Nancy.

"Who's what?"

"Over there—them." He nodded toward a couple sitting stiffly side by side near the fountain, almost directly beneath the gathering of naked Greeks. They sat sternly together separately, each tied in the twine of his own thoughts. Watching them awhile, though, I saw that the least little movement of one brought the quick attentions of the other.

"My oh my," said Arnold, "what a delectable little beauty she's become. Let's see . . . what's her name?"

"She's a virgin," said Cash with disgust. "Forget it."

Arnold's face lit up with delight. "No! Really? How about him? I know the faces but I forget the names. It's been so long, and he was a year behind me."

"I said forget it," said Cash. "Mary's a virgin and Harry might as well be."

"That's too good to be true," enthused Arnold. "The virgin Mary and . . . did you say his name was Joseph? Hmmmm. Meet the Holy Ghost! Listen, do you know what I want, my dear hostess? I want her for my main course and him for dessert!"

Cash was straining to remain placid. "Some wants," she

said in a long, slow breath, "are more reasonable than others."

"Yes, yes, that's very true, but we all want something, don't we," he said, leering down at her.

She looked like she wanted to belt somebody. "What's your friend want?"

"What's *your* friend want?"

Nancy and I were munching away at our sandwiches.

Cash wrinkled her face up and stared past me at Arnold.

"I have a hunch," said Arnold in a singsong chant, "that my friend wants your friend!"

Yeah yeah yeah, I wanted to shout.

"Now," he added, "what do *you* want?"

"Would you like to hear what your friend thinks of my father's collection? *Junk!* That's what he called it—*junk!* Arnold, much as I love and adore you, never never never impose upon my hospitality again by bringing something like . . . like this!"

A bite went down the wrong way, at that, and I went into a fit of coughing. Arnold was whacking me on the back as he went on talking. "Dear, dear Cash, I am, believe me, very sorry." Whack! "I'm embarrassed for both of us. He's a crude"—whack—"degenerate"—whack—"clod, I agree. I was only thinking of you when I brought him, though. Eh, what I mean is"—whack—"I thought you'd be pleased to meet an olympus prospect." Whack—whack! "I thought it would amuse you, darling. I meant no harm. And as for what he said about your father's most unique and valuable collection, well . . . he's usually a bit more articulate"—whack, whack, whack—"for all his boorish

54

stupidity and lack of breeding." Whack! "And, you know, we really should pity them. They've been culturally deprived." The whacks were becoming *whams!* "It's not their fault, really. And this one, well, I have known him to pull some horrible blunders"—*wham!*—"but on the other hand, he does, occasionally, evidence *some* promise. Eh, perhaps," he added reflectively, having given up pounding on me, *after* I'd stopped coughing, "it's that he sees things *symbolically,* so to speak."

Cash lifted her chin defiantly and looked up at him suspiciously.

"Eh, that is, you know, he sees things differently than *we* do. It can't be helped. You must be patient with them, you know. You must, there's no other way!"

"Arnold! It's *not* junk!"

"I know, I know—to *him* it's junk. The measure of his bad breeding and cultural deprivation. Very bad taste—atrocious! I've told him so a thousand times. Why, even as we were arriving today, I told him—I pleaded with him to please, please, at least make an effort!"

"Well, as far as I'm concerned, he's simply *wrong.*"

"Of course he's wrong. That's what I'm saying. That's why you shouldn't let it upset you, not in the least."

Cash stared up at him and munched a stalk of celery, and Arnold—thinking he'd softened her up—tried to score. *"I* know what *you* want," he said, leaning past me to look intently at her.

"You do?"

"Yes. You want him!"

I almost went into another coughing fit.

55

Cash looked past me at Arnold, her lips in a grimace and her eyes narrowed, like she was sure he'd lost his mind. "I most certainly do *not!*"

"Oh yes you do. If you didn't, you'd not be so excited. You want *him* to see things *your* way. Admit it!"

She let out a snide chuckle. "You know me better than that, Arnold—stop trying out your little debating tricks on me."

"Oh but you do, you do, you do! And now that you know what I want—well, remember how nicely we managed things last year?"

"Oh no, no more deals!"

He broke into his second favorite idiom: "Baby! Come on! Get *with* it. It's the most natural thing in the *world!* We just *give* each other a little *help.*"

"Not any more we don't. That's past."

He leaned past me again and, like an Arab conspirator to the American embassy, he said, *"You* need my help, dear friend, *more* than I need yours."

She glared at him. For quite a while she glared at him.

He said, "Everything's going to be just fine. Don't be upset."

"Who's upset," she said, nearly shrieking.

And with that, she got up and scrambled over our legs, up the steps onto the patio and away with quick, short strides, into the house.

And the next thing I knew, Nancy was following her in.

I said, "Hey, Arnold, when do we leave for the mountains?"

7

"WE'RE NOT GOING to the mountains, dunderhead. We're staying with this party."

"*With* this party! Are you kidding? You're not one of them and neither am I."

"Hmmm. Well, in that case, we must *strive* to gain acceptance—right? Now, about Cash—"

"It's a lost cause, me and that hostess. Nancy-baby—"

"For*get* Nancy-baby!"

"I can't, I—"

"I don't know how you *can*—I really don't *know* how you can make so many blunders in *such* a short time."

"Look, you had me all set to go to the mountains and then you throw me into this. What do you expect? Why'd you even mention the mountains?"

"To put you in the proper frame of mind for this party, oaf! I didn't mention the party because that would have made you feel inse*cure*. And you know what happens when you feel insecure—you *drawl!* What I've done, you pea-brain, is lead you to an opportunity, a mag*nifi*cent opportunity. *But,* you ungrateful mule, I can't *make* you drink!"

"Lookahere," I drawled, "what the hell you think Ah am? Some kinda pawn in yore game? That hostess you got in mind for me, man—she's somethin' *else*. I mean we don't even live on the same planet, me an' her."

"Listen—*listen* to you! Didn't I tell you she was *new-money?*"

"So?"

"So! What her dear old daddy needs—believe me, I know—what he needs is exactly what you will, as I so clearly envision it, become. A stockbroker he can *trust.*"

"I don't know a thing about stockbreaking."

"You'll learn. And from that humble beginning, and with my sure guidance every step of the way, you shall rise. Up by your own cruddy bootstraps like the mythical folk hero, bringing such honor to your own cruddy name —by bestowing it upon your father-in-law's only daughter —that *we,* I and the ill-bred likes of you, will be able to consort openly, associate publicly. You, dunderhead, will have become a person I can invite to my *home!"*

"Okay, I'm a stockbroker. I hereby bestow my cruddy name on Nancy-baby and take over *her* father's . . . what?"

"No no no! Dammit, man, *she's* a sinking *ship!* Stop being so dense and obstinate. This is your old Uncle Arnie talk-ing—believe me when I tell you that Nancy-baby's the sorriest kind of oldmoney. A string of weekly newspapers that'll be bought out any day now, and for just enough to set her paternal pumpkin up in retirement in some gone place like Geneva. He's not about to leave it to her or anybody else—he'll retire and enrich a platoon of medics, and when they've sucked him dry they'll simply let nature take its course, so *forget* Nancy-baby."

"But—"

58

"No buts. Hear what I'm saying—don't *board* that one for the ride up, dear friend—she's on her way *down*. You'll see what I mean. And don't worry about missing out. You'll get your cheap little thrill from her later. Later! In the meantime, you goof, the least you can do is look into the possibilities. My God, I begin to think you have a compulsion to failure. Every time I present you with an opportunity you either blunder or ignore it. What are you? Self-destructive? Can't you just spend a little *time* with the girl? The wedding's not today. And be*lieve* me, there's more going *on* here than has penetrated that thick, boorish, bumpkin brain of yours. So listen—listen to me for once, will you?"

"Okay. Let's hear it."

"Hear what?"

"What's going on here? Didn't you say you had a master-plan?"

"Had, yes. But your blunders have forced me to revamp and revise so much and so quickly, I'm practically back to start. The trouble is, you clod, the whole thing depends on you! You're the new element, my secret weapon."

"How's that?"

"You know how it works. A stranger comes into a gathering and brings a whole new mood into it with him. That's you, oaf—you're the new element here. Now, what it all hinges on is can you engage the interest of our dear hostess?"

"She's—"

"En*raged,* that's what she is. She did *not* like what you said about her daddy's things. Nor does she appreciate your

59

amorous attentions to Nancy-baby. For reasons you may or may not be aware of."

"She's in love with Nancy?"

"No, no, that's not what I mean. Anyhow, by now she must have you pictured as an utter demon, and knowing her as indeed I do, that means she'll have to sub*due* you. Which means I have no choice but to try to ex*ploit* this. Do you follow me?"

"Not quite."

"Well . . . I promise not to tell her what you really are, you everyclod. In return for which you shall endeavor to cultivate in her mind an image of yourself as potential riser up by your own bootstraps in need of the right young woman—her—for polish and refinement."

This motherfucker, I said to myself, talks like I'm a piece of low-grade merchandise.

"Ah ha!" he said. "I *have* it. You're *two* Randys. The only one our dear hostess has seen so far is Randy the oafish ingrate. Randy the prince charming has yet to emerge! He'll bowl her over with love and delight! Listen, it's just like that race you told me about—remember?"

How could I forget. Of all the warstories I'd ever told him from my tank campaigns, that one was his favorite. About a year and a half ago, I came up against a guy whose best time was half a second better than mine, so my teammate Jeff and I pulled a slicker. Jeff got himself announced as me and I got announced as him; he took the inside lane next to their number-one guy and we both went to working him over, to pull him off his block and unnerve him. We managed to pull him off twice, taking two of the three false starts allowed, and that put the poor guy down hard on his heels. With my rolling start I sailed out in front easy and ripped off a fine first lap. Then Jeff's next duty to our scheme was to take the guy out and pull his cork—to go the first hundred yards of the race all out, and with the other guy thinking Jeff was me, he felt he had to keep up for that first hundred. At the end of which Jeff's duties were done and he completely loafed the second hundred, confusing the guy beyond repair. All this time I was racing the clock with teammates yelling the splits to me on each turn, so I came in half a pool length ahead of this guy whose best time was better than mine. I hit the wall damn near passed out from the combination of exertion and hilarity, at which point our mistaken identities were officially corrected and the two coaches almost came to fisticuffs.

Ever since I'd told Arnold about it he'd been trying to figure out how to apply what he called the principle of the thing to his sport, lechery. But, for one reason or another, he'd never quite managed this, so now he was making me two Randys—and even though I protested that this did great violence to the principle of the thing, I had to admit I was a bit intrigued by the idea of metamorphosing from Randy the oaf into Randy the prince and winning the crusty-gold hand of our not-so-pretty hostess.

"But," I said, "how?"

"Leave that to me. Make your move when I give the signal, dunderhead, and until then, cool it. It's crucial to the whole party that you take over the hostess."

"Why?"

He took a deep breath and was, maybe, about to let me in on it when we were interrupted—Cash and Nancy-baby, both in bathingsuits now, were upon us.

Which I hadn't expected; they'd gone off in such a huff I supposed we'd have to woo them some before we'd get them back. But no. Here they were, big and brassy, and Cash was wearing—like it had just become the latest thing in facial makeup—a smile. It wasn't worn for me.

"Well!" she said to Arnold. "What shall we do?"

I forgot everything and blurted out, "Let's swim out to the yacht."

I was ignored. They chatted with themselves for a while and I watched the tennis match of invisible balls, until Arnold let me back into the game briefly: "My dear prince, aren't you going to put on your bathingsuit?"

"Oh, sure." I pulled it out of my back pocket and left them to go up to the boys changing room, a sheetless place full of overnight bags, clothes, towels, scattered all over. They'd been in such a hurry when they changed to their beach attire they just let their clothes fall off and plop to the floor.

Which I wasn't about to do. I went hunting for a hanger. I found a closet full of men's suits. Enough for a clothing-store show rack, but not one unoccupied hanger. I couldn't resist trying on just one jacket, but it didn't fit me so I put it back; I didn't have the gall to toss that fine suit on the floor and hang my cruddy old clothes in that closet, so I did the best I could—I folded my clothes and laid them down in a corner away from the general chaos, and then I paused at the door before leaving to chuckle at it—my faded old rags folded neatly and their bright new things strewn hither and yon and abandoned—though I wasn't sure who the laugh was on, besides me.

Then I went down to the patio in my most unfashionable nylon racing briefs, feeling exposed and vulnerable, and I stepped out into the sunlight to find Arnold, Nancy and Cash talking to another threesome, two girls and a boy. They took time out to introduce me around—Vikie, Vallery and Charlie—then went on with their chatter.

Charlie wanted to swim out to the yacht with Vikie. He was sitting with an arm around her possessively and Vallery was sitting on the other side of her, clinging to her by snuggling up close. Vikie was a brunette and Vallery a blonde, and they were about the same size and weight, and they were dressed exactly alike, as twins. But Vallery couldn't swim—that was their hang-up—and Vallery was saying that Cash had an inflatable raft, didn't she? And if she did, then they could get the raft and she'd get on it and all three of them could make it to the yacht—they could tow her there. This is just what Charlie did not want, and he didn't have to say so—it showed. What he did want was to shake Vallery and get Vikie alone. Well, Cash was trying to say that she did have a raft, somewhere, but she didn't know where it was, and that they were welcome to search the house for it. If they'd be careful not to disturb her father's things. So then Charlie wanted Vallery to go search the house, which Vallery steadfastly would not do; she insisted Vikie and Charlie come with her on the search. Vikie just sat pressed between the two of them, enjoying it. Finally, Cash said, "Well, if it's anywhere, it's in the garage. Come on, let's all go in and take a look."

So the four of them went—Charlie with an arm around Vikie and Vallery clinging close to her other flank and Cash leading the procession.

"Ah, love!" sighed Arnold. "What painful formations it doth cause. Come, let us repair to the beach."

And he put an arm around Nancy-baby and I clung close to her other flank, and down the steps we went in our own painful formation. When we got to the sand, I decided to take advantage of Cash's absence and Arnold's permissiveness, and I put an arm around Nancy-baby's waist. Arnold seemed to approve, for he was babbling on: "Is this not positively the most gorgeous, the most ravishing, the most superbly fashioned creature you have ever in your whole cruddy life laid eyes on, dunderhead?"

I allowed as how she sure enough was, for a certain, and was enjoying the whole bit—being tight with Nancy in this jovial threesome—when, suddenly, the temper of the times changed. Seems every time I got close to this girl *some*thing happened.

It took me a while to figure out what was happening this time. It was like the wind had shifted direction and changed the mood—until I realized that as we went in this direction toward the ocean we were collecting the attention of the others. They had no greeting remarks for us. Not one of them even spoke to us, but wow, what loaded looks. *Ah ha!* they seemed to be saying. Like there was something very important about us as a threesome and everybody knew what it was except me.

Well, back when we'd first arrived and Nancy'd been playing official greeter, singing out, "Boys upstairs, girls down," they had totally ignored her. Then there'd been that game of queen-dethronement and that strange hostility to her by those two bitches. And Arnold with his unconventional sexlife couldn't be expected to pull much buddy-buddy business out of them, and I was an outsider, a stranger and Arnold's guest into the bargain. But even considering all that and even some more odds and ends of our situation, it didn't account for the peculiar something in the way they were watching us. There was one foursome who'd been tossing a small hardball around—they stopped and stared. Then five or six who'd been batting a beachball around stopped and stared. Mean stares, like the whole scene was about to become gang warfare and I'd be smack in the middle of it not knowing what the fight was all about.

I leaned across Nancy's chesty magnificence and broke into Arnold's stream of charm chatter and said, "Hey, what the hell is going on here, anyhow?"

He put on a frown of perplexity, and then, as if he'd just realized what I was talking about, he switched on me. "Oh that's just some silly ball game—don't pay any attention to it."

But from the shallows was coming the rapt attention of the surfers now. Standing there holding their boards with their backs to the curling combers they'd been dealing with. The guy who'd said he wasn't one of them either—he was off by himself on a blanket, reading; now he looked up and stared at us. Even that couple, the Lovers, were taking a timeout, sitting up on their blanket, watching us like we were from outer space. All of them were.

Well, this business went on till we found a spot down near the water and spread our towels, sat down and looked around. Then, gradually, they got back to their various things. Or, rather, I chased their stares away by staring back, because quick as I'd look at one, he'd look away. I looked at the ballplayers and their game got underway again; I looked at the surfers and they took off out to sea; I looked back over my shoulder and the Lovers lay down and went back to their hardworking embrace.

Arnold, meanwhile, was staring down Mary and Harry. We'd put our blanket down about ten yards from theirs and Arnold was sitting there drooling over his main course and dessert. They sat side by side facing out to sea, with their knees up under their chins, looking very separate and lonely. Even distressed and in retreat, glancing every once in a while back at Arnold, like they realized instinctively that he was dogging them both.

Nancy was between us on her back, spread-eagled with sunguards on her eyes, worshiping old Sol. A pose I found enchanting; it put me looking back over my shoulder again to check on the Lovers. Were they, I wondered, alone among all these doers of things—were they merged by the magic of love? A successful matrimonial unit amid these glots and globs of disunity?

No. For it wasn't love they were making, I soon saw. It was more like a mechanical contraption. They were dispirited parts operating as smooth as a new hydromatic, like workers on an assemblyline enjoying the busy of their hands but disconnected from and unconcerned about the results of their work. Like ballet dancers moving through the motions without that one essential element—music to be moved by. Compared to the yin-yang of real lovemaking, they were competitors. I mean they were a sexless parody on the delights of sex. Loveless lovers.

Holy Hannah, I said to myself. No wonder that guy said I wasn't one of them and neither was he. Neither are *any* of them. There ain't no us here for anybody to be a part of. It's like each of Us here is a Them.

Back in the orphanage a bunch of us used to get up parties with a bunch of colored girls who lived nearby, and once the blast was on, we came together in a most unlegal oneness. Everybody there was one of our Us—once we all got with the rhythm of the music, we were all with the rhythm of each other. Because we were young, dumb and full of come, and all there for the same fun and games and couldn't afford to waste time by pretending we weren't, because making those parties was no small undertaking. First we had to figure out which house or apartment we could have it in, then there was a lot of cloak-and-dagger business to rounding up the wherewithal—the marihuana, wine, pornographic booklets and photos. Then we had to lay careful plans to make it into their territory and get away safely. We had to connive to get the bottles of wine and keep them hidden until the night of the blast, and then, when the housemaster put the lights out in the dorm, we'd get up, dress, dig out our bottles from here and there, and go sneaking over the grounds to go AWOL without getting caught by any of the nightwatchmen. Once out, we had the city police to worry about, plus the gangs of colored guys who'd run us down and take what they could from us—plus, we had to make it to the party without being spotted by any racist fathers, brothers or boyfriends.

Which finally did happen, and then there was hell to pay. Some chick's boyfriend spotted us and went and rounded up a raiding party. They crashed in just when we were all pleasantly tight together in the middle of the room, in the dark, dancing, high on marihuana, wine and the fleshier intoxicants, and they ran around the place yelling and swinging chains, brass-knucks and bare fists. Lord, how that housemaster's eyes did pop when he woke us the next morning and saw the bloody results! My bed was next to the door so the first thing he saw was the mouse on my cheek. Which was mild compared to what the others had suffered—I'd been the first in the mad dash out of the place, coward that I am. On the bed next to mine was the blood-soaked pillow of a fighter, a valiant warrior who'd taken on two or three of them while I was on the run. Next to him was another coward, but a slow starter—a goose-egg adorned the top of his head. And so on down the line. That housemaster spent weeks grilling us. Like he thought we'd had some sort of silent riot at two in the morning, or something. But none of us ever finked and so I guess he hasn't figured it out to this day. Even so, it was the last of our after-hours integrations with those fine females.

Anyhow, after all the conniving it took us to make those parties, we sure didn't put any blocks between ourselves and our goodies once we got there. Maybe, I thought, the difference is that these sons and daughters of the rich

68

and powerful got this party up so effortlessly. They came here in a breeze and if they can get free of their things, they can do with each other whatever they want to do. So what are they doing? Wasting time? Dreaming up difficulties? Maybe each of them has a masterplan like Arnold's. Maybe they're all trying to put difficulties to each other.

And right about here is when my other difficulty appeared—Cash, stepping gingerly down to the sand and coming toward us briskly, pacing stiffly over the sand, wearing her two-piece suit like an Easter bonnet, and carrying a bunch of towels cradled in her arms. Which she dropped on our blanket—on Arnold's side—and then she stood there stuffing her hair up into her bathing cap.

"Find the raft?" I asked.

"No," she said coldly, and looked at me like she thought it was my fault.

Then off toward the water she went and Arnold said, "Well? What are *you* waiting for?"

"A truce," I tried.

"Go on, she won't bite. You're all for swimming, aren't you?"

"Yeah, like I'm all for your game, too. If you'd only let me in on it."

"Them. That's all." Meaning Mary and Harry.

"Ha! That's too much. No room for *you* between *them*."

"Ah, but that's where the sport comes in, stupid. I have to *make* room."

"I think you'd better give that project up for a lost cause."

"Never. I'm the creative type."

"Some creation."

He held up a forefinger and reminded me, as if I could forget: "She's a virgin."

I quoted one of his favorite sayings: "And we must work to eradicate all innocence."

"Right, dunderhead. Take yourself for example—you're still not out of your cage enough years to know what's really going on in the world, are you? But forget that for now. We have here a greater innocence. See how frightened she is and how protective he is? She's having that big issue over her small tissue, you know, but she can't conceive of scrapping her vow to walk down the aisle in white. And him—Christ! He'd let his parts *rot* before he'd be *disrespect*ful. You see, all I'm endeavoring to do here is ease their travail, generous soul that I am. My problem is Harry—he's a frustrated deb escort. I really do believe he thinks love is next season's most publicized coming-out. I remember him from school—never knew him very well but he always had that deadly earnestness about him. I'm sure he'd lay down his worthless life in defense of the plaid cummerbund. So, you see, dunderhead, I must proceed with some degree of caution, no matter how generous my motives are. I may even end up having to work through *him* to get *her*, and you know I abhor doing it that way —it's so much like cheating, like carrying one's ball out of the rough. But you—your role here is so stupidly simple, and you do have so very much to gain. What's stopping you?"

Cash was standing in the shallows ankle deep with a hand to her forehead shielding the sun from her eyes and peering out to sea.

"I suggest," said Arnold, "a coeducational swim to the yacht. Immediately."

"What makes you think she wants to go?"

"Okay, then the thing for *you* to do is find out."

"You sending in the prince?"

"Not yet. I'm attempting to ready the situation *for* the prince. Go, dunderhead, and administer balm to those wounds that oaf inflicted."

Nancy-baby was propped up on her elbows listening to us, trying to figure out who and what we were talking about. So we shut up. She lay back down then and I got slowly to my feet. Making a move toward a ride to the thin air when Arnold declared the time was ripe had become an old habit.

Before I reached Cash, though, another girl almost collided with me as she ran by chasing the beachball, and Cash called, "Hi, Judy." And she kept her eyes on Judy like I didn't exist.

"How's the hostess enjoying the party?" I tried.

As Judy went cantering past us on her way back to the ball game, singing out, "It's an undisputed *flop*."

Cash smiled like the writing style of *Time* magazine, defensively haughty and cancerous. Then she put her back to me and was gone, off into the surf with an air of militancy, her shins churning water and the back of her legs showing the beginnings of ripples of fat.

So I wandered back toward our blanket, feeling relieved. Now, I said to myself, that motherfucker will have no choice—I have failed with the hostess, failed completely.

But he wasn't about to let me off as easily as all that.

71

He came to meet me halfway so we'd be out of Nancy's hearing.

"How many times have I *told* you—never, *never* be *hum*ble to the rich, be conde*scend*ing! Especially *new*-money!"

I turned sharp on him: "That's something you-all understand, isn't it?"

"Baby! Don't fight the good intentions of your old Uncle Arnie—you do have a thing about the rich, you know, and—"

"Like the thing you have about the poor?"

"Look, I'm only trying to guide you, to see you through so you can indulge your greedy, ill-bred appetites. Now what went wrong?"

"You tell me."

"If you'd only stop flexing your silly muscles and try to engage her interest—"

"There's no *hope* for it with her. Come up with a new masterplan."

"Dunderhead! Have I ever steered us wrong?"

"Yes. Now."

"Stop *fight*ing me. You didn't lose anything just then. The only thing that *bothers* me is you let her go so quickly—you let her *snub* you, you simpleton!"

"Dammit, you always get up some cat-and-mouse game like this. Let's just let it happen, whatever happens—for once let's just go along with what happens."

"Oh God!" he moaned, clapping a hand to his forehead. "You're even turning coward on me, do you realize that?"

"Always was a coward."

Which ended the matter for the time being. Arnold

turned and went back to the blanket and sat down, putting his old silent treatment on me. Which worked.

It worked on my orphan's complex, those insecurities. To lose Arnold's patronage and support would have been the end for me. At least, that's how I thought of it then. The straw that would break the weak spine of my half-baked ambitions to make it to the thin air. For not so long before coming to this party, I had faced up to the fact that I wasn't going to make it to the olympics—as a swimmer I was done, over the hill, and next season I'd be eclipsed by the young comers. I hadn't improved, really, since high school, swimming being a sport for the excessive passions of youth. When you lose that special moonstruck madness to put more than you thought you had into the race, you're done. On top of that sad fact of life, I'd already lost more than I had to lose, sooner than I had to lose it, in too many up-chuckings of Arnold's very good scotch. That, my only other means to my ambition—trying to keep up with Arnold—had already taken its toll, for the two efforts canceled each other out—each a dissipation on the other.

And there was no avoiding the fact that I was still a rag-tailed, awkward oaf among these overprivileged sons and daughters of the rich and powerful. They moved through a world they took for granted, which I stumbled through constantly astounded or jolted or embarrassed, never quite getting over the vague panic I'd first felt years ago when our motley crew of orphans went up against teams from the social altitudes and we found ourselves in those bright and shiny foreign lockerrooms among those seemingly gigantic, beefy, jovial, swaggering members of the Other

73

Team. Then there came that business about shaking hands before the race, just to show it was all a sport and counted for nothing, really. Which was absolutely not how I felt about it, since I'd realized very early that swimming was the way I might make it to some university, into my share of prominence and thereby on into the bigtime ratrace.

Those handshakes—wow, how I dreaded them. Even the race itself was only a prelude to another round of them, as if who had won—me—was of no importance, didn't count for a thing. The only thing that mattered was, did everybody get his hand shook and was everybody being ever so chichi, like it had just been an enjoyable frisky little morning dip at summer camp and never mind who won—*his* only reward was to get to start the post-race round of silly handshaking.

Well, this particular outlook on it had provided me with a goodly amount of the adrenalin I'd needed to be a winner, but the hypocrisy of it never ceased to put me in a panic, for it kept reminding me of the mysterious social snarl I'd be facing one day out there in *their* world, those big, beefy, blustering elegants who'd been born to reign, were already winners before that race began. Back in the orphanage we used to call them the cowboys, a reference to how brim-full of real milk they all seemed; the milk we got fed was powdered. "Hey man, we meet the soldier cowboys Friday." The military academy. "Yeah. You in shape?" "She-it. Baby, I was born in better shape'n them lardasses could ever *get* into." Said one scrawny runt to another. But if some cowboy had ever beaten me in those days, I don't think I'd have survived it. And Arnold, in some strange way having to do with his built-in

74

dream-reading radar, was aware of all this, even though I'd never mentioned it to him, for he always knew just when to badger me and when to shut up and let me badger myself.

8

So when Cash came out of the surf, there I was right handy, making the naked gesture of greeting her with a towel. I was overplaying the role, coming on scratch-and-shuffle humble—it was the only way I could think of to salvage a bit of integrity, or try to.

She accepted the towel like a bigassed duchess slightly perturbed by a moronic servant, and she dried herself slowly, with regal little dabs, while I stood by awaiting her slightest acknowledgments. Which were pretty damned slight—practically limited to picking the towel out of my outstretched hand.

When I realized she was going against my humble-pie routine so well it was backfiring on me, I came off it and said, "Hey, how far does this go?"

"Does *what* go?" and her tone hadn't lost its cutting edge.

"This beach. I mean how far can you walk before you, eh, run into people?"

"Miles."

"Yeah? Well, eh, gee, don't you get a little lonely out here?"

She chortled down her nose. "I *told* you, I don't *live* out here!"

"Well, I—"

"We come here on weekends and vacations, my father and I. Mother doesn't *care* for it."

"Oh."

"My father, you see," she said as she tugged her cap off, *"likes* the things in the house, *values* them. He'd like to *preserve* them—*and* the house."

I began to wonder if maybe she found Randy the oafish ingrate so bothersomely fascinating she wanted nothing to do with any other; after all, who else at this party had anything for or against all those sheet-covered things in her house. The others seemed indifferent to them—only Randy the oaf had feelings to match her own, and if his were the opposite of hers—well, maybe that's the stimulation she was looking for.

But my prince persisted: "How'd you like to go for a walk?"

That suggestion caught her by surprise, primed as she was to carry on the battle of the relics. After some hesitation, she said, "Okay," and it seemed we had shifted the basis of our relationship.

We went south along the beach, walking slowly over the wet sand near the undulating water's edge where the surface of the beach flattens out. For a hundred yards or so there was an uneasy, silent truce. Which I finally tried to capitalize on by breaking the silence with: "I guess I owe you an apology."

But that backfired.

"Why?" she argued.

"For what I said about—"

"Forget it," she said, unforgivingly.

I shrugged and concentrated on a group of clouds; they forecast rain and added to the atmosphere a lingering suspense that boded no good for the efforts of the other Randy. Still, he kept trying: "It's not a thing to forget and I want you to know that I'm sorry." But her argumentative tone was contagious—even the other Randy'd caught it.

"Look!" she said, pausing, bringing our stroll to a standstill. "Don't apologize to me, I'm not the house."

"You just *own* the house, eh." And now that oafish ingrate was threatening to take over again.

"My *father* owns it."

"And he likes all those *things* in it."

"Is there something *wrong* with that?"

"All those *things* out of the *past*."

"Exactly."

"I'll bet they're just great for . . . *living* in the past."

"Who lives in the past? We don't *live* in the past."

"Because you got the past so buried in shit. I mean *sheet! Under* sheet."

"I find your language dis-*gust*ing!"

"Shall we speak French?"

She ignored that, but she had those sharp brown eyes on me so hard now that I realized I'd come near the heart of something very touchy, so I stuck with it.

"It's your father who lives in the past, eh."

"Of course not! Who said anything about living in the past? What's all this about living in the past?"

"Well, all those things, they—"

"Oh! We *do* live with **a** *sense* of the past."

"I see."

78

"We build the future *on* the past, you know."

"Who? Which We is that?"

"What do you mean? We—"

"And what do *you* mean by *on* the past? Does this *we* just keep piling up, up, up? Sheet, sheet, sheet? Doesn't your We ever stop piling up sheet?"

"You're being absurd! You know what I mean—the future grows *out* of the past."

"Jack and the beanstalk."

By now, her face was flushed and her eyes wide with anger; she put her hands on her hips and said, like a shopper who's just been gypped by a salesman, "Well, if you don't like it—if you don't like the house or the things in it or me or this party, I'm *sure* we can arrange *some*thing. I'm sure *some*body here will be willing to give you a lift into town so you can catch a bus and go *home,* or where-ever!"

"What are you so mad about?"

"I'm not *mad!* I'm simply *say*ing!"

She was fuming, looking straight ahead down the long stretch of empty beach with her lips compressed into a thin, straight line. "My only concern," she went on with her jaw clenched, "is for the welfare of my guests—*and* Arnold's!"

She got the best of Randy the oaf with that. Not the reference to my being something of a partycrasher—it was that word "welfare" that got me. It made my teeth itch, brought back the taste of biscuits made from powdered milk instead of buttermilk, from flour out of the bottom of some surplus-food bin because her kind had no more use for Pappy.

79

She was in quite a rage herself. How all this business about that lesser British Museum big daddy kept up there under all that shit—I mean sheet—could make her fume and fuss so, I found that something of a wonder.

Anyhow, to try to save the situation, I made a big effort to send in my prince at his most charming; imitating Arnold's diction and style, I said, "You know, I really do regret that we've gotten off to such a miserable beginning. I really do, I really am sorry."

"Your sorrow," she said like I'd just handed her a dead rattlesnake, "is a waste of time—for both of us."

"Well, at least don't blame Arnold. He brought me here with the best of intentions."

She heaved a sigh at that and kept her face straight ahead as we walked slowly on. She seemed calmed down some now, so I tried a new tack; I meant to ease the situation by coming on countrified: "Yore pappy shore must be rich."

But that little feeler had a stinger on it for her too, and she bit back: *Fab*ulously wealthy!"

"Ah'm from the hungry side of the tracks myself," I tried.

"Don't be so smug about it; so was my father."

"Self-made man, up by his own bootstraps and all?"

She drooled sarcasm: "Id-i-ot!"

Rarely, if ever, had I aroused such keen emotion in a well-off young lady of such short acquaintance. Which, in itself, I was not at all unhappy about—but how in the world was that other Randy, that good prince charming, ever going to get a word in edgewise here? There was nothing else to do but keep trying, I decided. "Ah reckon," I tried, "that's why he likes t'buy up all them fine ole relics, bein' as how he's from the hungry side. You know, Ah allow as how that's somethin' Ah'd like t'do someday, if Ah ever got me enough money—buy up all them ole things and bury 'em under piles and piles of it."

"*Stup*id idiot!"

Which caused my oaf to slip out and come on hard: "Just think, if I was born rich I wouldn't have to be a stupid idiot! I could buy myself all the smart I'd need. Right?"

"*Fat*uous idiot!"

And that bent the oaf over with laughter. Somewhere in all her raw sensitivity over the matter there seemed a very funny victory for my oaf, and he couldn't resist roaring with laughter.

In response to which she grabbed my arm and spun me face to face with her and shouted into my oaf's laughter: "Look! It's too nice a day. You go *that* way and I'll go *this* way—so we don't spoil it for each other."

When she said "this way," she nodded at the stretch of beach ahead of us—she wanted to go on our walk alone, the walk I'd invited her on—she wanted *me* to turn back! And she didn't wait for any ands, buts or ifs, either; she stalked off doggedly, looking from behind like a hurt, stubborn, large-rumped child, leaving me with my glee-bloated oaf.

Well, that seemed like the end of an unhappy romance that would, happily, never come to be. I'd have to tell Arnold that that oafish ingrate just wouldn't cooperate, wouldn't give good prince charming a chance, and he'd just have to let me have my thing with Nancy.

In the meantime, it was indeed a fine day; those mackerel-back clouds were up there saying it would rain before this time tomorrow, but the sun was avoiding them and it was warm, sultry. So I decided to lay down on the sand with my feet in the swash of the more ambitious waves; I closed my eyes and let the oaf and the prince discuss the situation.

For he was in there somewhere, that prince, trying to make the oaf understand that there was justification for her anger, that if those odds and ends are silently chattering about that invisible set of assumptions we live in, our milieu, culture, society, civilization, whatever you want to call it, then her anger made some sense. Well, the oaf had to admit there was something to that, for he did indeed feel resentment toward those assumptions that put him at the bottom of the social pecking order and that richbitch up there at the top; especially since it did this for totally absurd and irrelevant reasons—namely, the circumstances of birth: she born to wealth and security, me to dick, if I can, the tricky cunt of fortune.

But, insisted the prince, that's no reason to resent her, to be rude and scratch her sensitivities raw instead of husbanding her hungers. Does being at the bottom bestow upon you some special privilege to be mean and nasty? Who's being mean and nasty? retorted the oaf. Dig how she comes on! Like, she's up at the top of all that junk, that shit her father collects, and I'm at the bottom of the pile. She's got all that crap piled on top of me and she's sitting up there, holding the whole works down. Goodness

82

gracious, said the prince, what an utterly self-serving metaphor that is! That's not at all how it really is, and you know it. If it's metaphor you want, forget the piles of sheet and try this one: it's a highrise apartment house and you and I are in the cruddy basement and she is in the penthouse, a lonely splendor. So, said the oaf, what's she expect me to do—*ooh* and *ah* and make pretty noises over all that highrising distance between us? Come *on,* baby! It's *cold* down here. Certainly, said the prince, that's why we should get out and go to the top, live in the penthouse with her. Sure, said the oaf, I agree. But how? Scale the greasy glass sides? Up by the bootstraps? Ah no, said the prince, ring her buzzer. You know how that works, don't you? Put the finger to her buzzer and ding-a-ling for attention in the penthouse. She pushes the button up there and that unlocks the door down here, and we're in. Hop in the elevator and ride right on up! Ha! said the oaf, talk about self-serving metaphors! Listen, if you get to that buzzer, let me know. Until then, shut up!

Then, suddenly, there was sand on my face and chest, and I was sitting up sputtering, trying to get it off my lips and out of my eyes, and when I looked behind me, there was Cash, wearing a snide mock-up of synthetic concern.

"Oh," she said, "did I kick sand in your face?"

I sputtered some more.

"Oh, I am awfully sorry."

Well, if she had decided to switch our styles, I had nothing to lose by going along with it. "Your sorrow is a waste of time—for both of us."

It put a faint smile on her lips, the only hint she gave about why she'd changed her mind and come back.

"I ought to throw you in the ocean and hold you under," I ventured.

"Ha! Think you're big enough?"

Which was invitation enough. I was up and after her and caught her after a short race, wrestled her up to a deadman's carry and went trudging out into the surf.

And just like that, the whole affair took on a new and different flavor. Out here on this vast, flat, lonely beach with the desolate and uncultivated land behind us and the empty sea and long sky before us all the way to the horizon, the hostile distance between us suddenly shrank to nothing. I tossed her into a wave, then went after her again, like I'd seen those three boys do from my rooftop lookout; I caught her again and hauled her out into deeper water. She was smiling impishly and trying to duck me and when we got out past the breakers where the rolling swells lifted her feet off the bottom, I let her overpower me and put me under, and as I was going down I slid under her, going between her legs, and put two hands around one of her thighs up far enough to make it meaningful, and I pulled her under with me. We went on with this sort of playing around for some time, and by the time it ended, we had replaced our earlier antagonisms with keen attentions to each other's bodies.

As we came sloshing out of the water, Arnold—in my mind—was congratulating me on the progress of my prince, and he was warning me to control that oaf now, and not let him grab at her crudely or make any rash passes. The way to handle it, he was saying, is to cultivate the affair's progress naturally.

But I'm afraid my juices had been a bit too churned up by this time—that thing with Nancy-baby before, and now the possibilities I'd explored in the water with Cash —and my oaf was nothing but grabbing crudely and pass-making rashly. Which took us on down the beach in a series of short dashes: I'd unhook her top during a bout of hugging and mugging, and she'd run away with her arms behind her back, struggling to do up the hook again; I'd come along at a jog, a slow jog—we were going south away from the house—and catch her after she'd re-hooked, and we'd go through the bit again.

This took us a long way. We wound up at a spot near the bottom of a cliff-like dune. There was a piece of drift-wood there, a board about a foot and a half wide, weath-ered smooth by the saltwater. I stood it up on end and we brushed the sand from it, then we put it down and it became our couch. We lay belly to belly with our feet toward the sea and our arms around each other, holding each other onto this island of clean wood. I unhooked her top for the final time and we spent the best of the after-noon debating with each other's more essential assump-tions.

What conversation we managed during this bout took on a tone lots friendlier than I'd thought possible with her. She was telling me about her parents and how they had decided they were bored with each other.

". . . so after they got the divorce," she rambled on lazily against my cheek, "I lived with my mother and I didn't see my father very much, but this summer I'm taking off from school and everything else, and I'm going to move in on him. I've already sent my luggage on to the apartment. I *am* his only daughter, whether he likes it or not."

And when she had thoroughly covered that ground, she asked, "Are your parents divorced?"

"Lord no!"

"Are they happily married?"

"They're dead. Got killed in an auto accident when I was twelve. Went off an old wooden bridge into a river."

"Oh, I'm terribly sorry."

"Don't be. The rest of the family's been taken care of —better than we would have been if they'd lived."

"My God! What an awful thing to say! Wasn't it a *good* marriage? I mean were there emotional problems?"

"Yeah. We were broke."

"Oh, financial difficulties."

"That's it, financial difficulties. We lost the farm and then Pappy got laid off at the factory."

"Laid off?"

She said it like she'd never heard the term before. "The company became so efficient they no longer required the fruits of his labor."

"But . . . how did they manage?"

"Who? The company?"

"No! Your parents."

"Oh. Not so well. Badly, in fact."

"Well"—and now the gulf between us was really getting wide—"did he look for other job opportunities?"

"There was only one factory in town."

"I mean somewhere else, some other town."

"When times are good there's no reason to leave, and when they're bad, you can't. No getaway money. We were

86

stuck. If the two of them hadn't gotten themselves killed, we'd all still be stuck back there."

"But . . . what happened to the rest of the family?"

"Well, there were three younger than me, and they got snatched up by people for the foster-care money. My older sister and I got put in orphanages."

"*Tisk!* I *am* sorry to hear that.*"

I was tempted to tell her again not to be, that it got the rest of us out of the country slum, out of that old economic masochism, but I was enjoying her sympathy too much for that. Besides, I got to thinking of my youngest brother, Allen, and how he got put with some old farmer who worked him sunup till dark, until he rebelled, lost his head and took after the farmer with a pickax. That got him put away in a reform school and he was still there. Beth, she got married when she was fifteen and I spent time with her and her husband in their housetrailer; he fixed me up with a job my first summer out of the institution, and I stayed with them until I went to the university that fall. Susie and John landed in pretty good homes. Every once in a while John fires off short notes to everyone, telling his marks in school. He has a teacher who's putting into his head bigger ambitions than he knows what to do with. His notes read like applications for a Fulbright filed by a disenfranchised braggart. Susie I lost track of; she dropped out of school when she was sixteen and left her foster parents. That was two years ago and no one's had hide nor hair of her since, so we figure she must be doing okay.

I was the pride of the litter, having swum myself a long, long way from home. Up the creek far enough to be sniffing the wellsprings. Only because I'd been put into that orphanage where the major sport was swimming, where we had a Yale grad—our coach, father figure, hero—a saboteur of the system who treated us not like we were waifs lost at the outside of it all but like we were the salt of the earth and had damned well better get cracking and show it. He used to keep a recordplayer blaring during practice and when we got lazy, he'd get a disgusted look on his face, take off our music and put on a slow waltz, swivel back in his chair, prop his feet against the wall and pretend he was giving it all up, going to sleep. To bring him back, we had to make that old tank echo with the roar of our combined hard-working churnings. We won an invitational meet that put us up with the best clubs in the country, and the Monday practice after that meet, when we showed up in our usual sweatsuits—but expecting a celebration— all he said was, "Okay, you ragged-assed orphans, warm up with jumpingjacks. Ready, one . . . two . . . one . . . two." And it was only the way he looked us over as he put us through the same old grind that let us know what he was feeling inside.

But I didn't go into all this with Cash; she hadn't been the first richchick to develop a curiosity about my past and I had learned during my two summers out among the swim-club set that to tell them too much of the story was to strip the mystery bare and give them an image of me as Levening Lumpenproletariat, when what they really wanted to relish was their assumption that I was a fallen angel. The backward, waydown, welfared, automated-out poor they preferred to worship from afar.

Anyhow, that's how we passed the afternoon—getting

88

acquainted. That is, giving each other versions of ourselves
we hoped would meet with acceptance, laying on that board
with our bare torsos together, the smallest movement facil-
itated nicely by the big ball-bearing action of her mushy,
pink-tipped tits.

9

SHE DECLINED to bring our joys to their natural culmination right there and then but I was down-home dumb enough to be feeling ahead in the game when we decided to knock it off and go back. We walked back with the sun low and the wind getting chilly, with our arms around each other and in step with the outsides of our thighs together. Dark clouds obscured the sun and now the air held the hint of rain. When we neared the beach in front of the house, the wind was rising and shifting, hitting us from off the ocean and kicking up whitecaps and globs of foam, blowing us damp.

Thing-doing had come to a halt and the guests were in groups. Most of the girls had their hair up in pincurlers and were sitting in a circle, and most of the boys were huddled around a guitarist and were singing good-night-ladies-type songs, and their collective attention was on Nancy-baby, who had just departed the blankets of Arnold and was passing them on her way to the house, lumbering along in her bikini like a farm girl sloshing through mud —until she realized the attention of the singing boys and then her posture straightened and her pace quickened to the short, girlish steps of that other side of her personality. Arnold was left alone on the blanket and was lying very still, as if asleep, but with his face toward Mary and Harry, who were still side by side, gazing out to sea. The yacht lay at anchor with its bow into the wind; the outboard had been beached and four guys were toting the sailboat's hull away and one followed them bearing the mast on his shoulders. The Lovers were disengaged; she lay on her stomach listening to the singing boys and he sat up staring at the circle of girls. Here and there lay waterskis and surfboards, stranded like the forgotten toys of children.

The girls were sending us glances from their circle that suggested they were discussing us. Then Judy girl clown broke from them and came scampering through the shallows to intercept us. She came to an abrupt halt in front of us, put her hands on her hips saucily, cocked her head to one side and said, *"Are* we to go the *rest* of this party *dry?"*

"Heavens no!" said Cash.

"Then shall I do the honors?"

"Please do. You know where everything is."

This dispatched Judy at the same silly scamper back through the shallows; at the circle of girls she cut and went skipping through it, going next to the boys and becoming a choir director briefly by waving her arms at them before she went on toward the house. When Cash and I reached the circle of girls, one of them sang out, "Say, Cash, I don't believe we've met your new friend."

So Cash put through introductions, a lot of ordinary names I promptly forgot, and they sat there looking up at me something in the manner of livestock judges, cold and curious. Some turned on smiles like sneers, and a few ran their eyes over me disdainfully, like they found even the sight of me slightly distasteful—me, the outsider who'd come as the guest of the notorious Arnold, who'd taken a quick, firm, forthright interest in the shunned Nancy-baby and was now to be seen in a coziness with the hostess. It had me feeling downright notorious.

I was all for going to the house and getting warmed up after the introductions, but Cash said, "Let's take one last dip."

"It's too *cold!*"

But she took my hand and pulled me along. The way she was going about it—under the arch, down-the-nose gaze of her girlfriends—I realized she was putting on for them, trying to prove something. I wasn't sure what, and I wasn't easy about it, but we went anyhow, splashing into the surf, and we were frisking around in the breakers, handling each other like a couple who've gone together a long time—all for the benefit of that circle of the pincurled. Who, finally, broke circle, shook out their blankets and towels, and went in one large flock toward the house. Then Cash decided we'd had enough of the water for one day and we sloshed out, found her two towels and went to rubbing ourselves down hard and fast, shivering in the strong wind.

Now most of the guests were gathered at the foot of the steps to the patio; they were watching Judy bring a cocktail table on wheels down the steps. The big bowl of martini and the longstemmed glasses perched majestically upon it and she lowered it carefully down each step like a baby carriage. She made it to the beach without a catastrophe and was given a short *hooray* by the others, then she tried to push it along further but the wheels got bogged down in the soft sand, so she gave up and parked it.

Judy was tightly surrounded by the gathering and everyone was grabbing a glass and holding it out to be filled, but Judy got to prancing about behind her bar, humming and doing a heavy-footed jig in the sand to the theme song of a TV cartoon. She broke this off as Cash and I arrived, and she set to dipping out glassfuls of martini and firing off such cracks as, "Would you like a dry martini or a wet one? Hey, son, where's your draft card? You know we don't serve minors here. Well, okay, if you're old enough to die for your country, you're old enough to destroy your liver."

I kept an arm around Cash like she was my ticket to their midst; I had the sensation of being at some new kind of masquerade party and was trying to act my part the best I could. I squirmed an arm between some naked ribs and picked us up a couple of glasses, then held one at a time up and out, there to meet Judy's dipper and get filled as whole mouthfuls of martini slopped over the elegant rim of the glass onto the heads and shoulders of those in front.

As she worked at her ladling, Judy kept saying, "Hold it, wait a minute, don't drink yet—don't touch that drink until I give the word! I have a toast to make!"

And when she'd gotten all the glasses filled and an ice-cube dropped into each, she stepped back from the bar and raised her own glass, and she called, "Attention, attention, everybody."

Then, coming on as a potbellied Rotarian type, with

93

her thumb under the strap of her bathingsuit like it was a suspender, and in a hammed-up imitation of a pompous Babbitt, she went into a speech: "Yes-sir-ree, all the world's a stage, somebody said, and I'll go along with that. But what I want to know is, where's the prompter? The one who keeps cuing me to do things I don't want to do. Say things I don't want to say. Where is he? Why, if I find that . . . that . . . I'll haul him before the House Un-American Activities Committee! Yes-sir-ree-bob! Cause he sure is a menace!"

Then she went into a little strut and gazed about, gauging her effect on the others, overplaying the stiff-necked after-dinner speaker. "Hold it, hold it," she called to someone, "don't drink yet, I say—I'm not finished."

But the natives were restless. "To Judy's prompter," said the one with the guitar, "may he provide her with many, many lines."

"No no no—wait!" shouted Judy, scurrying about with her glass held up gingerly, trying not to spill too much martini while she unbent their elbows and got them to listen. "Don't drink yet, dammit!"

She got their attention and went on: "I don't know how your prompter is, but mine's a son of a bitch. He makes me go to bed on cue, get up on cue, eat on cue, speak on cue, shut up on cue. I mean there's not a damned thing I do that I'm not doing on cue! As a matter of fact, I'm going home—later on tonight, sweetie, in the wee small hours—but I'll be going on cue. I'll be going home from college just like I went away to college—on cue. Just like I went to kindergarten on cue, to grade school on cue, to junior high and to that silly girls finished—I mean finish-

ing school on cue. I learned on cue what I wasn't the least bit curious about, and I *didn't* learn what I *was* curious about—I didn't get cued to. But I graduated, all the way up, *on cue*. Hey, you know what? I even took my mother's milk on cue—she told me so herself, all about the schedule the doctor put her on. And so it only stands to reason that I'll get married on cue, get pregnant on cue, have the baby on cue, raise it on cue, get cancer on cue and die on cue. There'll be a funeral on cue with people crying on cue, then they'll drop me into the ground on cue. Ladies and gentlemen," she intoned gravely, "I do hope you find it in your hearts to join me—on cue—in this toast: to the prompter!"

"Judy-baby," said one large, pudgy, crewcut heavily, "if I ever find your prompter, believe me, I *shall* convey your sentiments."

"Find your own prompter," said Judy.

And there was a round of sipping, then we all moved up the steps to the patio and went hunting for places to sit down out of the way of the rising, chilly wind. Cash found an abandoned blanket draped over a deck chair and we wrapped it around the two of us and sat huddled together on a bench with the planter wall protecting us from the wind, and I was sitting there pondering Judy's toast, for it did make me keenly aware—again—of the difference between me and these others.

I'll do away with both Randy the oaf and Randy the prince for the time being, and I'll have Randy the mayor proclaim it. Whereas, in the country slum I'd lived in till I was twelve I knew of the commands, sometimes loud and clear, sometimes implied, of the managers of our

95

society, of those from the same class as these I now partied among; and whereas later, in the orphanage, I'd gone to such great lengths to evade their rule, cheat their intentions, disobey them and prevent them from reducing me to thinking of myself the way they thought of me; whereas my life, or a good bit of it, had been devoted to evading *any* promptings, their lives had been, would go on being devoted to installing into the involuntary muscles of their psyches a prompter, like a pre-programmed computer that jibed with a sort of central prompter outside themselves— their source and creator, their inherited wealth and power; therefore be it resolved that I, in order to beat them at their own game, must go on resisting, evading, disobeying what their prompter will prompt them to have me do, be, believe —what they will feel they *should*, because they will be doing, being, believing what they feel *they* should, unquestioningly.

Well, maybe not unquestioningly—Judy's wit had gotten to some of them, I noticed. Some of *them* sat pondering too. Maybe they're on the verge of realizing that they're being transformed into highclass ticky-tacky to rule over the rest of the ticky-tacky in that great stagnation that grows profits like stagnant ponds grow algae.

Come to think of it, maybe it was Judy's wit that fertilized the seed, that rebellion against the state of Should that grew up and bloomed into the big scene of regurgitating souls. But that comes later.

Right now, there was a rush on the two showers and changing rooms—boys upstairs, girls down. Judging by the noise that was coming from the girls shower, it was large enough to take care of two or more of them at once, for

96

they were advertising their sociable showering loudly, teasing the boys who waited their turn in the one-at-a-time stall upstairs.

The first one to turn up primped for the nighttime leg of the party was Nancy-baby. She'd been in the shower during Judy's toast and now she came gracefully out of the girls room in her hiphuggers, and she went to great lengths to avoid us—Cash and me—as we sat huddled together in the blanket. She looked to the right and left of us, never at us.

Some of the boys had carried Judy's stage prop, the rolling bar, back to the patio and put it down near the table which held the buffet. Nancy went straight to the big punchbowl and got herself a drink, and was dipping her glass full. She was so close to Cash and me that she had to know we were here, so when she kept refusing to see us, I said, "Hi, Nancy."

Then she made a big show of finding us and sat down —beside Cash—just about the time Arnold happened along, wearing his blanket Indian fashion, and sat down next to me. And here we were, a fearsome foursome—the hostess, the two ostracized and the outlander—sitting silently at the poop-out end of the day, sipping martini from these elegant longstemmed glasses, with the mainstream members of the party all around us, drinking and waiting to shower, going, coming back dressed and primped. The four of us didn't have a thing to say to each other, but they—those Should people—they were a-babble with all sorts of greater and lesser announcements and debatings. Jumbled tidbits of which I cocked my ear to hear.

A curly-haired guy with glasses was saying, "I don't

97

care what the majority opinion is, I don't think we'll *find* life on Venus when we get there." Like as if Venus is a dead whore.

Over in one corner a small glot of them were having their classical agony. "It'll collapse of its own weight!" shouted a lopsided-looking guy. "Oh no," yelled a roughneck. "That's a myth. The truth is, we're in a fight to the end. We'll either break the worldwide communist conspiracy or die trying. *Because,*" he said with his eyes wide and weirdly gleaming, *"they* are fanatics! We *must,*" he bellowed like a teenaged Don Quixote, "make the world safe for *free*dom."

I could imagine him a few years from now giving the order to push the button to free us all from existence, for he was, as they say, dedicated.

"You've got to make a responsible decision and take a position and make a commitment," insisted some guy from the far end of the patio. He sounded like he was suffering and his face was scrunched up, like whatever he meant by a commitment was going to be a tight squeeze for him.

"Of *course* Shakespeare didn't write those plays," said some foxy-looking chick. "Why, he lacked a firstclass education!"

And a tall, lean, lank bitch in short shorts was saying, "Well, she wants to take her last year in Europe but her analyst's in Boston—she'll just have to sacrifice."

There were the two high priests of their very funny faith. "Automation *creates* jobs," said the one. "Of course it does," said the other.

Then there was that one chick who kept tonguing the rim of her martini glass. She was saying, "Oh *you* know, it's one of those *dirty* books—sex-sex and *more* sex. I mean it's really very *bor*ing."

"Women are people too," said another daughter, a voluptuous, scowling blonde.

"He's a tre*men*dous talent," exclaimed the classics fan. "Practically a genius. Plays Beethoven's Violin Concerto."

And closer by, there was a debate on about my people, being had by three guys. "That's just what they do not understand," said one. "The great thing about America is it's a mobile society—you can go up and down, up and down in it."

Which somehow made me think of fucking the scowling plump blonde, until the second guy said, "Yes, but welfare saps their initiative—that's the tragedy."

"No, that's not the problem. The problem is their *morals!* They don't even have *time* for anything else, not even a good education—they're too busy *breed*ing!"

"But we can *lick* that."

Which made me itch.

"Yes, think of all the new contraceptives we have now."

These motherfuckers don't need us any more—they got machines now—so it's like they want us to cease to exist. They call it the population explosion and say it's a problem. But they were saying more:

"I still maintain it's the giveaway that's ruined them. Why should they go out and look for a job when they can sit on their fat asses and collect our money."

Said the fattest ass of the three.

"And the *Neeg*-grows, all *they* want is to have everything, just *handed* to them." Said the tightest ass. "They go around putting on all those demon*stra*tions!"

"Well, let's try to be liberal," said the fattest ass, and I strained my ears to hear this. "Here's the situation," he lectured. "We have all these countless people"—and right here I was very tempted to pop up and ask the mother-fucker why he didn't count all these people his *we* had—like his *we* count the money, don't they? But he went on: "We have people who can barely read and write. Is that *your* fault? No! Is it *my* fault? No! Then whose fault *is* it? It's *their* fault. They and their parents. Let's face it—*some* people just don't *have* it. Won't *work* for it like *we* do—*our* parents. I mean it's only human nature. You have the kind of people who *do* things, and you have those others, the kind who want to sit back and profit on somebody else's labor. That's what the income tax is all about—*we* support *them!*"

Dig that shit, I said, almost out loud. Wow, what an echo from the far side of the great American mythology! What the next civil war will be over—which *we* are "we" going to put away in those concentration camps their Mc-Carran Act set up. And if that's what his *we* has in mind, it sure does cut down the choices for me and mine. It means we'll have to imitate these bastards in order to fight them. Adopt their ways and become as despicable as they are in order to overcome them, and that's a deadly contradiction. And it's all because they popped out of particular wombs to find they "own" us, and now they're saying to us, Stop living, we don't need you any more, we got computers now. And if we don't feel like giving up living, they give us some funny choice: we can become them to join them or become like them to fight them.

Now ain't that a pisscutter? I mean how well they can tell themselves stories that leave out where their wealth comes from.

Well, these thoughts had me tensed up, but the fight wasn't tonight and in the meantime, here I was again, an English-speaking idiot studying metaphysics in Vienna, a spectator at the tennis match played with invisible balls. These motherfuckers got the rest of us living in their delusion so bad they think their delusion is reality. And, well, it is, since they get to name the game—it's the operating reality of our lives. So I guess that makes it reality. For now.

And there I was sniffing these stinking tidbits of their Shouldly concerns when suddenly I got jerked to my feet by Cash, who lurched to hers and said, *"Oh!* I have to call my *fa*ther! I promised I'd call before *six!"*

And we went as a pair in a blanket into the house, around the aquarium that was now a-dazzle with colored lights, into the kitchen area to a wall phone where she dialed and I slipped behind her.

While she talked I was having my way, first with the zipper of her bathingsuit bottom and then with her essentials. And if it hadn't been such a struggle to keep the blanket up around us, I might have lost my head and done the trick, defeating my purpose—my purpose at that time being to make it *her* idea, later.

From what she said into the phone, and from the honking it gave back, I gathered that her father was loud with worry over the welfare of his things.

"Yes, Daddy, the party's on the patio. We're only using

two rooms—the one at the top of the main stairway for the boys and the apartment bedroom for the girls. Otherwise the party's strictly on the patio."

Then some honk-honking, and: "Not one *thing* has been touched!"

As my kneading fingers made squishing sounds between her legs.

"That's not the party you hear, Daddy. It's Mrs. what's-her-name, she's making hamburgers."

"Well certainly! They have to go into the house to get to the upstairs room. They can't very well climb up the outside of the house, *can* they."

"Daddy, believe me, everything's outside on the patio. We're going to charcoal hamburgers out there, *eat* out there, *dance* out there, *stay* out there till the party's *over!*"

"*Please,* Daddy! *Stop* making such a *fuss!* It's just a simple little stop-over on the way home, the same as I had last year and the year before that. Remember?"

"Daddy, you *know* you shouldn't drink gin. You *always* get this way. Promise you'll switch tomorrow—vodka, scotch, *any*thing."

"Yes, I'll be there tomorrow before noon. I'm sleeping here tonight. Did my things arrive?"

Mrs. what's-her-name, the caretaker's wife, was about four yards away as I worked Cash over under the blanket, and she was—I discovered about halfway through all this chatter when I glanced back at the reference to her—turning scalding black mammy eyes on me. They met mine, then dropped to the blanket activity at hip level, then met mine again. In response to which I looked disdainfully down at the ground meat her fingers were kneading, then back at her.

I tend to believe she read me, for she came off her angry auntie, and though not a word passed between us, after Cash's telephone call ended and we were struggling to get zipped up and shipshape again, I caught the dark eye once more and this time it was coy. Like giving me the okay, just as long as I kept to my own end of the sugarloaf.

Cash and I went, married in our blanket, to stand just inside and watch the goings-on for a moment—the collection of current jukebox hits was on again, blaring out toward the ocean and being blown back by the wind. Most of the guests were still sitting around in small debating societies, sipping their drinks and concerning themselves with Shakespeare's lack of a firstclass education and the shiftlessness of my kind, and I was all for going back to sit in on it some more. But Cash wasn't, and like the obstinate one of Siamese twins, she marched us through the main room toward the front of the house, around and under an arch and down a short hallway to a stairway back there. Up the stairs we went with our hands all over each other, and I was so sure now that good prince charming would soon ride tall in the saddle, I was carrying on a Shouldly debate with myself and the shiftless no-account I am. Should I or shouldn't I worry about contraceptives?

No. I had nothing to lose and a contribution to maybe make them, so I decided my duty was to the fire and to hell with whether she was on pills or what—that was her lookout.

My lookout was to make sure I put it to her good and

proper, so she'd damn well remember it, and so as we busily climbed the stairs I was giving myself a peptalk: I'll make her beg for it, I'll rub it up her cunt lengthwise and round widthwise, and get every millimeter tickled and teased; I'll blip her clit up and I'll blip it down, and I'll blip it east and west, and when she's about to scream for it, I'll deliver—I'll work it in real slow and busy, with circular motions and triangles, clit-leaners upwards and wang-twangers downwards; I'll stroke so slow and nice she'll panic on the out strokes and glory on the in strokes, and when she's getting ready to come I'll jam it home so big and bad she'll think it's the Dixie sunshine come to melt the Alaskan snow, and she'll come like a Russian thaw. No matter what else happens, she'll never forget me as long as she lives.

Then we emerged on the second floor and she led me into a room full of ghostly piles of sheet; we climbed onto the sheet-covered bed and took to tonguing, fingering and stroking each other's sensitivities. My tank trunks had been on the floor a good while before I realized she was out to prevent me from sending my Dixie sunshine north. In fact, she wasn't even going to take off her bathingsuit—lastex went on covering the nub of the problem and no matter how shiftless and immoral I became, no matter what lengths I went to to reach her more down-to-earth emotions, she was bound to draw the line at what they call petting. It wasn't long, then, before this scene had me very edgy, for I still had ringing in my ears that phrase: "The problem is, their morals."

Well, the thing sort of came to a head: I had one hand

104

down under the lastex with a finger on her buzzer so strong it should have raised holy hell in her penthouse, and the other hand under her back, trying to get the zipper all the way unzipped, when she said in a chill, wintry tone that sounded like walking on dry snow: "What do you think you're doing?"

I'm doing just what you brought me here to do, rich-bitch, I felt like saying. But instead I just quietly gave up. I pulled my one hand out from inside her lastex and the other out from under her back, and I made a big thing out of sniffing my finger. Which caused her to giggle.

It's their morals, I told myself. Then she handed me my racing trunks and said, "Behave yourself."

And right about here, I'm afraid I wouldn't have be-haved *her*self if she'd begged me. Which she of course wasn't about to do, for she was sitting on the edge of the bed, puffing a cigarette and watching me stuff my rejected conviction back into the confines of the nylon racing trunks. She seemed to think this was a gas; she said, "You *are* having a difficult time, *aren't* you." Like reassuring her-self that the whole scene was ending in discomfort.

"Come along," she said, "we'd better get back to the others." She picked up the blanket, hugged it to her belly and led the way out of the room. And so it came to pass that instead of impressing myself upon her memory as I'd been planning to do, I ended up trailing along at her heels like Pappy's most faithful and stupid beagle hound. I could almost feel my ears flopping as I made my way downstairs behind this sweet flower of American woman-hood, and I emerged at the bottom of the stairs wondering

—almost out loud—what the hell a shiftless immoral no-account like me was doing breaking his ass to be had by the likes of this.

Oh yes. I remembered—the ride up, Arnold's masterplan and all that.

But, good lord, if the rest of the trip's as bumpy as this, it sure must be a kidney-buster.

"Wait here," she ordered when she got to the edge of the main room. So here I was, in a dark shadow at the end of the aquarium with my conviction conspicuous in my nylon trunks, while she went to the patio to check the party.

Out there, I could see, colored lanterns now hung from wires overhead and a glot of them were in the middle of the patio gyrating to the electric guitars.

Then, while I was waiting, two girls came inside jabbering furiously, and as they turned toward the kitchen, I overheard, "That's what *any* woman wants—a *man!*"

And an irresistible urge drove me out of the shadows and in front of the aquarium's colored lights tugging down my trunks and presenting my credentials—the firm, upstanding essence of my manhood—and I hollered, "Hey girls! Lookahere!"

They did; then they shrieked in unison, turned and raced each other back out to the patio.

"Hypocrites!" I yelled.

In response to which Cash came back in through another door, came padding over the hardwood floor to where I stood tying the drawstring of the nylon trunks. "Everything's fine," she said with a cheerfulness I found disheartening. "But *we're* the only ones who haven't had a *shower!*"

Forthwith she bestowed upon me a privilege: "Say! How'd you like to take *your* shower in the *girls'* room?"

I was struck dumb.

"It's much better than the one upstairs."

I opened my mouth but nothing came out.

"Well? Oh come on, don't be bashful." She took me by the hand and led me past the dramatic dazzle of the aquarium and into the bright white lights of the girls' room, a place littered with bathingsuits, overnight bags, pocketbooks, bras, panties, dresses and wet towels, everywhere—on the floor, the two beds, chairs, doorknobs— and all smelling of perfumed soap and hinting of the clean warm bodies of the anywoman who wanted.

"Go ahead," she said, "you first."

I remained stock still, thinking how much nicer it would be for us to go together, instead of me first. But before I could offer this suggestion, she turned me around, put her hands to my back and pushed me into the bathroom, closing the door behind me.

Well, it wasn't for lack of space that she hadn't come along with me. This bathroom was about the size of the house I'd lived my early years in. It was a network of bathrooms in a bathroom, this bathroom. To my immediate left was a bathroom that housed a commode and washstand; in the middle of the main bathroom was a showerstall big enough to accommodate half a dozen; in one corner there was a little alcove that housed a bidet; toward the rear there were two washstands built over a row of cabinets in front of a long mirror. In the other corner there was an area of tiled splendor upon which, as on a throne, sat a sunken tub. Truly, I was a long way from that pride of my childhood, our family's sociable two-seater outhouse. I was in a huge, bright, gleaming palace of plumbing!

And so it was horrible beyond the telling of it to learn, when I stepped into that room in the middle of the bathroom and turned the magnificent, ostentatious shower handle—to learn that there was no hot water left!

It was a comedown as disgraceful as one that had befallen me the summer before when I was going with one of the richbitches from the swim club; her girlfriend was visiting this one particular weekend, and her girlfriend's boyfriend was in town, so the four of us went out on Saturday night in this chick's daddy's bigass Cadillac convertible. Well, the night had a rousing beginning—with me standing on the sidewalk in front of my humble summer digs and the three of them rolling up in this big Caddy, me hopping in behind the wheel and off we roared —in such a glory I was sure I was out of some movie they hadn't made yet. We crossed the state line and went to this joint that has a homegrown semi-pro group that's a boomer and we got ourselves a table front and center and we danced. The other guy, a West Pointer who was nevertheless surprisingly human, got quickly swacked and spent a good deal of the time vowing to quit the Academy and get married.

Going home, the other girl drove and I got in back with mine, who had drunk herself giggly by then. I hoisted her onto my lap with her legs astride me and about halfway home I decided it was pants-off time. Which almost became a catastrophe, for she was going limp on me and I had to lift her up to get her pants. The car's top was down and when I heaved her up off my lap, she almost kept going right out of the car. Like maybe she had her libido mixed up with her deathwish, who knows? Anyhow, I got her pants and put her astride me again, and now she was aroused enough to be wiggly as well as giggly, and between ministering to the core of her wiggliness and trying to get my pants unzipped I had my hands full for the rest of the trip. By the time we pulled into her driveway, she had her head plopped down on my shoulder and had become a complete rag doll. But I was to a point where she could have been half dead—I wanted mine. And I had just about maneuvered her foundation and my conviction into the right position for meaningful dialogue when I felt a strange and overpowering *heat,* like somebody'd just stuck a little potbellied stove between us. A hot chick? Well, I said to my drunken, half-numbed brain, *no* chick can be *this* hot! And, sure enough, I soon realized that this heat was *wet.* A wet hot. This dear daughter of the rich and powerful had gotten hers on the way home, had tuned out then, faded, let go—and she had *pissed!* On *me!*

There then followed a bad scene: I shoved the front seat forward, opened the door and pushed her off me; she went tumbling out limply to land and sprawl on the macadam of her driveway. She was completely out. The couple in the front were aroused now and wondering what was going on, so I stood up on the back seat and showed them my wet britches. "Look!" I yelled. "The bitch, she pissed on me!"

The girl didn't know whether to laugh, cry or hit me with something, but the cadet, he roared and we couldn't get him to quiet down. As for me, there was nothing left to do but get out and walk the two miles home with a short step and a galling, chafing stagger.

Well, that trip upstairs with Cash that had ended down here under this cold water in this outlandish showerstall was akin to that time I'd started out behind the wheel of that bigass Caddy and come home pissed upon, and neither the girl from the summer before nor Cash now seemed aware of my humiliation—the one had passed out and the other had done with me pretty much as she'd wanted to do. And never mind what I'd been presumptuous enough to expect from either.

I came out of that shower transformed—shivering and not at all happy. Hot piss from one and cold water from another—if they were half as good at pleasure as they are at frustration, these rich girls would be very fine indeed. But as things stood, it was almost enough to discourage any high riser by his own bootstraps. About all I had left was the fervent hope that this party would be going into some final turn and I'd come on hard in the homestretch and get them in the end.

10

THERE WASN'T A DRY TOWEL anywhere in the bedroom, so I ended up rubbing myself down with somebody's absorbent pajamas. Then, in a walk-in closet, I found an elegant silk bathrobe, bright yellow and covered with Japanese pagodas; I put it on and headed for the patio to rejoin the cocktail hour.

When I slid open the door and stepped outside, there were guys sitting in a row on a bench by the door, and I was expecting them to crack wise over my very fancy robe. But they ignored me. One of them was holding up his elegant longstemmed glass and was peering through his martini at the colored lantern overhead, and he was saying, "Tonight I'm gonna stay sober."

"Ha," said a second.

"What for?" said a third.

"What can you do sober that you can't do drunk?" said a fourth.

"Okay," said the first, "you talked me out of it."

I moved on. A few couples were in the middle of the patio dancing with movements like those old-fashioned threshing machines—mechanically competent but jerky— and some little discussion groups were still in session. A group of five girls stood jabbering over the tops of their martinis, and cocking their heads, trying to keep the wind from undoing their hairdos. The music throbbed and vibrated and the talkers gesticulated and the dancers gyrated jerkily, and the whole scene was splashed by color from the lanterns which swung on their wires in the wind and sprayed their mixture of hues this way and that.

I saw Arnold approaching as I ladled myself out a martini; when he reached my side he fingered the robe and said, "That's her father's."

"You see? I'm already taking over."

"Where is she?"

"Isn't she out here?"

"No, dunderhead, and neither is Nancy-baby."

"Wayll," I drawled, "I guess that tells the story, the fate that has befallen the valiant prince charming."

"Come on over here," he said, tugging me along by the sleeve, "I want a full report."

We carried our drinks to a couple of aluminum deck chairs at the seaside end of the patio and, much in the manner of middle-aged chaperons, we leaned back, observed the goings-on and chatted. Which began by my telling him, as eloquently as I could, how kidney-busting, ball-breaking, back-aching, hot-pissed-upon and cold-showered were my efforts to become a riser up by the bootstraps, and that if the present trend continued I would have no choice but to crap out, get off, go back to my own immoral and shiftless kind, where at least most of the anywomen feel *some* response when confronted with the reality of a firm conviction, some response other than to leak upon it hotly or shove it under cold water or run away

112

shrieking, and that I was a bit fed up with certain styles and customs I found among the well-bred, elegant sons and daughters of the rich and powerful.

At the end of which report, Arnold threw back his head and said, "Ah, poor, poor Cash!"

And that about finished me off! I was sucking in a lungful to let him have it when he went on:

"You must have patience with her—she's a house divided against herself. She's like that . . . that . . ."—he waved his martini at the house—"she's in one hell of a dilemma, one foot on the brake and the other on the accelerator. I mean she has this perfectly ridiculous habit of going to the brink, tempting the fates, then trying at the last minute to stem the tide. All this attention she's giving Nancy-baby, it would be completely beyond me if I didn't know them so well."

"I don't know them at all," I ventured, "but if they ever go slumming, they'll be very, very ridiculous."

"Now now, don't be nasty about these contemporaries I've chosen for your glowing future. Listen, dunderhead, in the months that have elapsed since I saw her last, Cash has shifted the emphasis of her attention in two very telling ways: she has become absolutely fanatical about the things in that house, and she has become likewise about Nancy. Maybe she's in love with Nancy and won't admit it, won't have it out."

"That's a thought for you to think," I said. "I thought that at first but now I think she's just frigid."

"No! Consult the appendix. When I brought you here, you oaf, I aimed you straight at our dear hostess. Who'd just *love* to get her claws into a highriser by his own bootstraps. But *you,* you goof, I couldn't get you past Nancy-baby, and I'm not sure which angered Cash the most—your ill-bred attitude toward the glorious trappings of our superior culture or your hard-on for Nancy."

"Nancy's the only human here. The rest of them are fashion-magazine cutouts."

"Dunderhead," he said with some pleading, "will you do me a favor?"

"What?"

"Shut up. Shut up and let me think."

So I shut up and tuned him out as he rambled on about how I should have left Nancy alone and not have let Cash get away. And my mind wandered back to a time during my teens when a church charity sent some of us to a summer camp and we'd gone for a hike one day to a lake. There was a fleet of rowboats and canoes there, and the counselor said we each had a choice—either a rowboat ride or a canoe ride. He went down the line and each boy named his choice, but when he came to me, I said, "Both!" He said, "You can't have both—pick one or the other." But I didn't see anything wrong or outlandish about my choice, so I stuck with it. He said, "What are you, crazy or something? You gonna stick one foot in a rowboat and the other in a canoe?" That got the others laughing, which put me down and out. What I'd wanted was to go awhile in a rowboat then switch with somebody who was in a canoe. But I ended up sitting on the grass beside the lake watching the others paddle around in rowboats and canoes—I got neither.

"Hey, goofball, are you listening to me?"

"No."

"Well, what I'm trying to do is find the significance for us in the parallel."

"What parallel?"

"How she adores her father's collection and it's under wraps, and how she adores Nancy-baby and now she wants to keep *her* under wraps too. Which is where *you* come in, dunderhead."

"With pleasure—I'll unwrap her first chance I get."

"No no no! How many times must I say it? You must keep Cash *away!* Get her mind *off* Nancy—*then* it'll happen."

"What will happen?"

"You'll see. It's all a matter of proper timing, and that's *my* responsibility. But will you promise to take care of Cash?"

"Sure, sure. When she comes back. I can't take care of her if I don't know where she is."

"Good. Fine. Now we're—"

"But how's that get you what you want?"

He leered broadly.

"Anyhow, where are those objects of your jaded lust? Have we lost track of them too?"

"Oh no, they're right over there." He nodded to where they sat with that brave, tortured patience—across the patio on a bench against the planter wall, side by side, as stiff and uneasy as ever. I allowed myself to hope that they'd escape Arnold and make it past the barrier of Mary's cherry and get to their rightful goodies, and do it soon.

Then somebody at the recordplayer lifted the needle from

115

the electric-guitars disk that had been wailing out at us and slipped on a collector's item, a 1920s-sounding dance band that came out scratchily with a crooner groaning:

"I can't give you anything but love, baby.
"That's the only thing I've plenty of, baby."

The half-dozen who'd been dancing to the guitars rushed the machine and snatched off that one and reinstated their sound.

Arnold was rambling now, on a binge of compulsive talking about these contemporaries of his—how he'd grown up with most of them, had gone to prep school with every one of these guys who to the man were snubbing him, avoiding the both of us. And the funny thing about it was that, at the same time, they were also trying to be ever so hip and cosmopolitan, as if they thought of themselves as fashionably dressed neo-bohemians, like they'd wind up the night with cool jazz and a poetry reading. For his part, Arnold felt as if the flimsy wings of his grim gay had flown him far past any point they'd ever get to, so this made the snub mutual. It also, I supposed as I pondered the scene, took him away from that need the others felt to carry themselves with that certain chin-up, straight-backed, graceful stiffness. Arnold slouched as much as me—he slumped down in his chair, or bent over and put his elbows on his knees, or rested a foot on the planter wall, flipped cigarette butts backward onto the beach, and continually leered at the others as if he found no end of amusement in their goings-on.

Then he said, "Hey, watch this!"

116

And he departed, sauntering in his lean and hungry Arab way over to where Mary and Harry were sitting, on the bench nearest the naked stone Greeks. They did their best to ignore his approach.

Now he was standing directly in front of them with one hand propped against the hip of a Greek damsel and the other holding his drink, and he stared down at his prey in a waiting, vulturous way. But Mary and Harry acted like a couple on a bus being stared at by a drunk, like they didn't want to encourage trouble by even noticing. They kept their heads lowered, eyes meandering over the patio's deck, and Arnold was standing over them quite awhile before Mary gave it up and raised her face to him. He waved his glass at her, as if to toast her, and some words passed between them. Then Arnold set his drink down on the rim of the fountain and went into the house—to a group of unpedestaled statues clustered just inside the door, as if waiting their turns for more permanent resting places in the house. He whipped off the sheet and picked up an Aphrodite who'd lost both arms and legs, and he carried her out and presented her to Mary and Harry. More words passed between them, then Arnold wormed his Aphrodite between them and put it down on their bench, making it a threesome.

He left, then, and was walking back toward me; they came to their feet and were shuffling around, not sure whether to take offense, take the Aphrodite back inside, or go find themselves a new bench to sit on. Then Mary went off—suddenly she just walked away. Across the patio and into the girls room, leaving Harry standing there gaping. Arnold saw her depart before he reached me; he watched her go into the girls' room, then he turned to Harry and stalked him.

I was too curious now; I got up and wandered over to try to listen in. I was trying to be inconspicuous but I only put more worry into the heart of Harry, who saw me coming and stiffened like he was afraid Arnold and I were moving in to beat him up. I pretended the stone Greeks were the object of my curiosity and was fingering them, standing behind Arnold and trying to hear what was being said.

"Did *I* do something?" said Arnold.

Harry didn't answer.

"Where *could* she have gone?" said Arnold.

"Who knows!" said Harry fiercely.

Which didn't discourage Arnold at all. "You know, all day I've been trying to remember. You weren't at last year's party, were you?"

"Sure I was," said Harry, looking disgusted and turning away.

"Oh *now* I remember," said Arnold. "Yes, and you were very good—you played football, didn't you. Yes, yes, you played *end!"*

Which almost cracked Arnold up with laughter as he said it, for he had all sorts of double meanings for team positions and sports events.

Then Harry cut the scene short by walking away and pacing about in front of the buffet table, casting expectant looks at the girls' room. But even this didn't turn Arnold off; suddenly, in a loud voice, he announced: "Say, I bet

I know where she is." And went past Harry at a brisk pace, disappearing into the main room.

Harry paused a moment; he glanced toward the girls' room, then toward the main room, and finally he felt compelled to follow Arnold.

I strolled, as casually as I could manage it, over to where I could see into the main room; they were standing on either side of the fish aquarium, looking into it and pointing.

My God! Surely Mary couldn't be in *there!*

I backtracked to the door into the kitchen area and managed to make it around the partition to the kitchen out of Harry's sight. Then I looked around the end of the wall and saw Arnold through the seaweedy water of the tank, looking like some primordial being trying to talk to the fish inside.

"It is *not,*" said Harry. "It's just a common ordinary goldfish!"

"Really?" said Arnold.

"Certainly. Can't you tell?"

"It's pretty."

"Pretty *fat,* if you ask me."

How Arnold had driven Harry's attention into the fish tank I never did figure out, but the diversion was shortlived. Interrupted by a sweet voice saying, "Hi. What are you doing?"

And there was Mary; she'd come out of the girls' room by the door into the main room, I guess, and walked up to them from behind Arnold. There was chattering and questioning; Arnold dripped solicitously about hoping his little prank with the Aphrodite hadn't upset her and she went overboard to assure him it had not. Then Arnold got to chattering about this group of statues on the floor just inside the door, trying to pin their attention on this and hold them. He lifted the sheet from other pieces there and was talking a museum guidebook at them.

But Mary hooked an arm around Harry's arm and maneuvered the pair of them out the door, leaving Arnold to re-drape the statues like a sidewalk toy demonstrator who'd just lost the last of his audience.

I was coming on him from the other side of the aquarium anxious to seize this opportunity to rib him—when from out of the girls' room stepped Nancy and Cash. Nancy seemed distracted and a bit pouty; Cash came on smiling and pointing a finger at me, laughing a short hard laugh at the sight of me in her daddy's bathrobe. Which sight amused Nancy not at all; she stood gazing out at the dancing on the patio.

We exchanged where-were-you talk, then Arnold shot me a leer that said, "Sic 'er, prince!" And took Nancy-baby out to the patio.

The jovial spirit Cash was in now didn't help me at all.

"Well," she sighed happily, "*I* still haven't taken *my* shower." She snapped the lastex shoulder strap of her bathingsuit top and, giving me a big broad coy look, turned and walked away swinging her hips. It struck me like gloating over how she'd shoved me under that cold shower, and I was giving myself a lot of reasons for not following her, when she said, "And I'll need that robe." Then went into the girls' room, poked her head back out, and smiled.

120

So I came along obediently and went straight to the nearest bed and sprawled out on it. She was opening and closing bureau drawers, hunting for something, and she was saying, "That Arnold—what in the world did he *say* to that poor child?"

"What poor child?"

"Mary! She was crying like a baby! Over her vir*gin*ity! Can you imagine!"

Well, yes, I could. "Arnold is cursed with mental telepathy," I said.

"My *foot!* He thinks he's . . ."

"What?"

"Never mind."

And she went padding into her cavernous bathroom and shut the door between us.

I got up and turned out some of the glaring lights, then fell back down on the bed and concentrated on relaxing completely. I was feeling weary and a bit frazzled in the nerves, and the rest felt good.

The bathroom door opened a crack, sending slivers of bright light into the room and whiffs of steam rising. I cursed softly to myself. A cold shower was fine for me, but she waited till there was hot water again. What homemakers these daughters of the rich and powerful must be, my poor-boy's prejudice growled.

Then she called out in a silly singsong: "Will you do me a favor?"

I felt like saying, I sure will, baby. Bend over and I'll de-bitch you.

But instead I silly-singsonged back: "What is it?"

"Run upstairs to the hall closet—it's the fourth door down on the right—and get me a dry towel."

What was it that guy'd said about America being a mobile society? Up and down, up and down. So up I went and down I came with the sort of towel I'd have cherished after my visit to her palace of plumbing. I went then to that majestic structure's portal and I pounded undomestically, loud and hard. It peeped open and her bare arm came slithering out with fingers licking the air.

"Where *is* it?"

I couldn't resist; I opened the robe and guided her groping fingers to my limp conviction. "Here!"

"Randy!" She said it like she'd touched 120 volts. "Oh! Oue! Ick!" She yanked her arm in and slammed the door. From inside, like a soul tormented, she hollered, "Will you *please. Give* me the *towel."*

What a tremendous response, I thought. My conviction brings more out of her limp than it does firmed up for duty!

She was still in there yelling for me to hand her the towel, huffing and making noises of outrage. "How can I give you the towel if you won't open the door," I suggested.

"Well . . . none of your stupid tricks."

And this time she poked out just her hand, its palm up commandingly, so I hung the towel on the end of her middle finger and she clutched it in and wham went the door again.

Toilet training.

About two months before this party I'd encountered a guy I knew in the university library; he was reading a book with a title like "The Problems of Toilet Training," and was being bowled over by it, wanted to talk about it, said it was amazing how much impact early toilet training and such has on later character development. He wanted to know if I could remember back that far.

Well, yes, bits and pieces of it. When I was old enough to perch over the smaller hole without falling through, my sister Beth would escort me to our sociable two-seater and we'd grunt in two-part harmony. She later told me I had a keen knack for identifying, by peering down the hole, who had been there recently, and I eventually developed this knack to such a degree that my announcements on visiting Sundays had sent uncles and aunts into gales of laughter. I couldn't recall amusing the kinfolk, but I could remember that Beth and I went steady to the outhouse for a long time, and that these occasions had been pleasant, what with the business of look-what-I-have and lemme-see-yours.

And besides this atrocious lack of proper toilet training, Beth and I were also bed buddies. Nobody'd ever told us we shouldn't be and so we were—snugglers par excellence, playing the doublespoon back and forth, first me to her back, then turn and she to mine. I'd venture to say we developed the toughest doublespoon in the whole house; I'd go so far as to say it could rank with the best anywhere. We could even fit little Allen into it and never lose a thing.

He was everybody's favorite, Allen; for a year or so he was nothing but a rounder, crawling in with you at any hour, proving himself the most talented cuddler in the house. Then he settled for Susie, for reasons known only

123

to the two of them, I guess, and with Susie's regular, John, it made that scene a threesome. So when our parents suddenly decided to put me in bed with John and Allen, and Beth with Susie, everybody rebelled. Allen won the day for all concerned with a tearful tantrum over the loss of Susie and Pappy finally allowed as how maybe it'd be okay, for just one more year. And by that time, Beth and I were to a point where we'd wake up in the middle of the night full of such wrigglings and squirmings we'd do each other what they call violence—we'd make vigorous, unorgasmic love till we got tired and went back to sleep. Any way you cut it we were dreadfully shiftless and immoral.

Well, standing outside her palace of plumbing now with the door slammed in my face, I was a long long way from home. I'd just decided to go lay down on her bed again when the door peeped open and shed those tile-reflected bright lights on me once again; I turned and she was standing there with the towel around her, her face stern, lips in a tight, straight line.

"If you please," she commanded with an arm extended to me.

She wanted her daddy's robe. So I opened it and was taking it off when she turned her back, stomped her foot and huffed angrily: "Oh! Honestly!" And dashed back into her palace again.

Truly it was most fascinating. I mean here we were with all those naked statues—that circle of stone Greeks outside—and the feel or sight of me in *my* altogether made her act like a Baptist who's been ordered to attend synagogue. Even with my deep-rooted prejudice against the rich, this dashing-away and door-slamming and back-turning—and

124

after that session we'd had upstairs—these reactions were becoming a bit *much!*

Again her door opened, and this time her head poked out, and she snapped: "Well! Don't just *stand* there. Put something on!"

I was tempted by the possibilities of that command, but I let it go. I just picked up a big wet towel and put it around me and went on back upstairs, pausing at the top of the stairway to lift the sheet and tweak the nose of the Roman emperor there, and went into the boys room and through a deeper chaos of overnight bags, wet towels and bathingsuits to my neatly folded clothes, thinking that if I was going to make it with any kind of win out of this sorry soiree tonight I'd damn well better get cracking. Then I stopped by a mirror to inspect my overly laundered chinos and faded pullover shirt, and that put me to wondering if, all things considered, I'd better just accept the loss, that the odds were too much against me here.

Downstairs the girls' room was dark and empty; Cash was out on the patio, circulating graciously among her guests. There was a lineup for food by the table again, and another disagreement at the recordplayer—the classics fan feeling it was high time he got to put on one of his and the dancers telling him that classics were great and all that, but. It ended with the dancers reestablishing their jukebox numbers and the classics fan stalking off disgruntled.

I diddy-bopped through the midst of the gyrating dancers putting on I was the spirit of Sammy Davis, and went over to see Arnold and Nancy, who were sitting alone near the steps to the beach. But Nancy stood and turned her back on me. She leaned against a smallish copy of "The Thinker" that decorated that end of the planter wall, and I found myself confronted with her pretty rear and "The Thinker's" solemn head.

Plus the sparkle of Arnold's bared teeth as he leered into the wind-tossed colored lanterns. I was about to ask him what was going on with Nancy, when he said, "Hey, watch this!"

He brushed by me and I swung around to find Harry and Mary strolling past. Arnold caught Harry by the arm and said, "Harry, how about popping off with me."

Well, Harry stared at him for a second, then he reared back, cocked a fist and let fly a haymaker. Arnold ducked and moved away howling with glee as Harry went down, almost, from the follow-through momentum of his punch.

"With *this*, Harry, with *this!*" yelled the delighted Arnold, holding a tiny capsule up between his thumb and forefinger. "My *God*, man! What *is* it with you?"

The scowling Harry regained some composure, moved a step closer and peered at what Arnold was holding. "What's *that?*"

"It's a kick, just a kick. It counteracts the booze."

"What *is* it?"

"Who knows? But boy, what it *does!* I'm glad you didn't have a whiff before you swung on me, you'd have knocked me into the next world! Harry, you're so *strong*. Why did you swing at me like that? Do you feel hostility toward me, Harry? Harry, I'm no threat to you. Believe me, I mean you no harm. Why, I think you and Mary are the *sweet*est two people *at* this party!"

Mary, now, was tugging at Harry's arm, trying to rescue

him from his interest in the tiny capsule. Arnold, in an attempt to hold his interest, cracked the capsule, and held it up to his nose, inhaling deeply. Harry leaned forward anxiously, watching for some sort of reaction. Which Arnold gave him—he reeled backward in a well-executed swoon, bumping into Nancy, who turned and caught him and eased his way down to the bench. And then, like from the edge of this fantastic high he was supposed to be in, he tossed the capsule to Harry. Who caught it, eyed it, waved it around in front of him at a safe distance from his nose and sniffed cautiously; he frowned and wrinkled his nose, then tossed it into Arnold's lap and said, "No thanks." And Mary hauled him away.

Arnold straightened up, picked the capsule from his lap and tossed it backward over the wall and onto the beach, and said, "Shit."

It was just some kind of smelling salts.

"You better give them up," I said, "you ain't making it."

"Don't underestimate," said Arnold, putting on his leer again. And then he quoted from my swimming liturgy: "Pace yourself right and you'll suck out his heart on the last lap."

I cringed.

11

AND BESIDES CRINGING at that butchery of
my liturgy, I had something else to cringe at—how cold and
withdrawn Nancy was being. Was she mad at me? Or was
she just in some dumpy mood? For some reason I'd jumped
to the conclusion that she was in on Arnold's masterplan
and knew I was only hustling Cash as my contribution to it.
Well, if she wasn't in on it she should be, I thought, and
she should be hip enough to know that somewhere toward
the end of this strangely tense party, she and I'd just have
to get together and finish what we'd started upstairs earlier.
So why was she behaving this way—turning away every
time I was around?

And while I was standing at her back and wondering
what it was with her, she split—went strutting away in
her hiphuggers and bikini bra looking like she should be
shivering with a chill; she went to the end of the food
line and there she stood with her thick dark hair responding
to the breeze. She was pretending to be oblivious to the
others but they—one glance around the patio showed me
—were anything but oblivious to her.

And now there was becoming something about the mood
of this party that reminded me of Little Cousin Norman

and his fear of sinkholes. A very sensible fear, come to think of it. Norm used to tag along after the rest of us when we were youngins and he was what Pappy called knee-high to a big thought, and the only way we could shake him was to holler: "Sinkhole!" At the sound of which word Little Cousin Norman would take off chop-chop at a chubby little scamper for the house. And now—watching this weird, sinister attention to Nancy-baby's body in the food line—I felt like Little Cousin Norman, and like somebody far away was hollering, "Sinkhole!" I had an urge to run off and hide somewhere.

And then I noticed the wind had died down. No more playful gusts; it was just an easy balmy breeze now, and the whole scene was like suspended, hung on the smell of rain, like charged with some unreleased energy. It showed in the way the boys stared at Nancy-baby. As if they were mad at her for having such an appealing body. And the girls were sitting back, watching, like waiting for something to happen. And then Arnold—he was giving the whole scene his keen attention too, and watching every self-conscious move Nancy made.

The food line was moving in fits and starts as hamburgers were grilled by the half-dozen and plopped onto paper plates, and salads were dished up into wooden bowls. The dancing was at a complete standstill; one boy who'd been thrashing away faithfully was left standing there with sweat running down his face, looking around for a partner. He found none, and near him, his buddy—a chunky, muscular guy with kinky blond hair—was so rapt and hang-jawed over Nancy-baby's body that he was forgetting to eat his

129

hamburger; he held it up ready to bite but instead of biting he was just staring. As Nancy, ignoring all those hot eyes, moved herself up in the line and got her plate filled.

"What's *this?*" Judy said loudly from the far side of the patio, pointing a finger down a row of girls. "Tryouts for a Rolaid ad?"

It was a glum lineup. Some of them had finished eating and were just sitting, watching, waiting; even the ones who were still chewing were hung-up, spooked. Even Judy, I'd venture to guess, was spooked, for she was trying too hard to liven things up—the hardworking high priestess of poo-poop-a-do.

And now that the wind no longer swung the colored lanterns, her father's Greeks had a new look. They were like spectators who had just arrived from out of the night and were standing there in the semidarkness at the edge of it all, wondering what was going on. I had enough booze in me to imagine their reaction—to see, by the way the soft lights shone on them, their sly smiles. I put words into the mouth of the nearest stone lad: "What are they up to here? Some practical joke?" And the nearest stone girl replied: "Shhh! Maybe it's a religious service of some kind."

You're both wrong, I thought back at them. And maybe, in a way, you're both right.

Arnold was sitting with his legs crossed, leaning forward smoking, staring down at his burning cigarette thoughtfully.

"I've never seen it like this," he said.

"Like what? What is it you are seeing?"

"Nancy-baby—she's so re*pressed!* After her third martini

130

she's usually beating a path in and out of the nearest bedroom, taking on all comers."

I clapped a hand to my forehead. *"Now* you tell me!"

"What?"

"Why didn't you say something before?"

He shrugged. "Do I have to paint you a picture?"

"No, but you can at least tell me what the hell is happening here. In plain old American, just tell me, tell me."

"Don't you *know,* dunderhead? You were the one she was going to debut with. Remember?"

"What do you mean?"

"You goof, it was you who screwed up the timing, broke tradition."

"How?"

"By dragging her upstairs before lunch. Or can't you remember back that far?"

"Well, sure, but—"

"And that, as it's turned out, I see, was your all-time blunder. I didn't realize how much of a blunder it was, until now."

"There must be a lot you didn't tell me, Arnold."

"I suppose so."

"Well . . . ?"

"For instance, Cash has been trying to convince that poor girl she's a nymphomaniac. Now, that's an illness, and she wants Nancy-baby to either get over it or seek help."

"Who's ill?" I said, mostly to myself as I gazed around at the others.

"Of course it's not an illness, dunderhead. It's an evil! And in order for this party to go, there has to be some evil. Good emanates from evil. It's very, very necessary.

Without it, all is lost. I ask you, dunderhead, how am I going to get set up for my own goodies if Nancy-baby won't do her part? My God, she's let herself be so brainwashed by Cash that she's breaking tradition! Right before our very eyes she's breaking tradition!"

Then the lineup of girls Judy had tagged tryouts for a Rolaid ad caught my attention. They all sat leaning forward expectantly now, reminding me for all the world of a group of cheerleaders I'd once seen going by in a pre-game parade —sitting in an open convertible, in a semicircle around the back of it with their feet on the back seat, waving their arms, bobbing their heads and all chanting: "Gotta*win, we *gotta* win! Gotta*win, we *gotta* win!"

There was that pre-contest feeling everywhere, like waiting in a lockerroom with butterflies in the stomach. The boys were in loose huddles, each lost in his own contemplations, either staring square at Nancy or glancing over at her every now and then. And suddenly gone were those touches of polite flippancy, that counterfeit, store-bought uppity air. There was an intensity you could practically see in the air, and could damn well see in their faces. I sat there feeling my heart pounding, wondering what they were fixing to do, now that it was pretty clear that Nancy had broken tradition. Would they burn her at the stake?

Because there definitely was the hint of something murderous here. It was like the time, my first summer out of the orphanage, when my brother-in-law had gotten me a job on the highway, and one Friday night, instead of going straight home, we stopped off at some dive he knew. We had a couple of sandwiches and we drank; the night wore on and the atmosphere, as that joint began to jam, turned

132

tense, just like this party, on the edge of something blood-thirsty you could feel. Maybe it was the combination of people there that night—the men in their workclothes fresh from the grunt and sweat of dishing up their labors, and the women, a couple of housewives out on the town, a few white pickups and two colored hustlers from some other town. And there was this one big barrel-chested man-mountain with a bad eye for everybody who was standing at the bar chasing down his bourbon with beer—in some silent gutrage over God-only-knows what in particular. In general, he was mad at the world and the rest of us there that night were his world, and the bad eye he was giving out caused the gutrage to spread like a disease. So when some old clod accidentally-on-purpose bumped into him and made him spill some beer, old badeye up and took after that clod like a mad bull with a torch at his ass, and by the time he caught and almost killed him, the whole place became like a ward for psychopathic killers. Before the dust had settled, the white hustlers ganged up on the two colored ones; one nut was leaping around with a broken bottle cutting anyone he could reach; one old duffer was off by himself in a corner shadow boxing; the bartenders had run for cover and four or five huskies were using pool cues to smash bottles behind the bar, and I had felt wound up enough to join a mob which started by trying to separate the man-mountain from the clod and ended in a free-swinging celebration of our own individual angers. I left the place in an ambulance, went from the hospital to jail and lost my job on the highway; my brother-in-law got away clean, hopped in his jalopy and got his cut arm bandaged by my sister in their housetrailer. The upshot

133

was, my sister blamed me! I had to sweettalk her for a week to keep from being tossed out.

"I'm afraid," said Arnold, "that what I'll have to do is act as advertising counsel here. Otherwise this party may never get off the ground."

Cash was inside. Nancy was sitting by herself, eating.

"Arnold, tell me—in plain American tell me what the hell is going on here? I mean, are they waiting for her to lay down in the middle of the patio, or something?"

"What an artless dolt you are, dunderhead. No, they're not waiting for her to lay down. It's just that she's so strangely inhibited. She's not herself at all. It's confusing."

"Well, what's happening?"

"Nothing! Nothing's happening—that's the trouble, you pea-brain."

Then he stamped out his cigarette and said, "See you later." And he got up and strolled through this thick stillness to where Nancy-baby was and sat down beside her.

The least I can do is give it a try, I thought. So I followed and sat down on the other side of her, and while she nibbled her hamburger and Arnold talked softly, soothingly to her, I just sat, hoping she'd dig that I was presenting myself as an alternative.

She acknowledged my presence by turning slightly away from me and leaning closer to Arnold. And the next thing I knew, here was Cash, sitting down beside me, scowling, tight-lipped, grim, like maybe she thought I was trying to help patch her broken tradition, instead of getting Nancy to myself, all to myself.

"Listen," said Arnold, leaning around Nancy and leering

at Cash, "don't *wor*ry. It's a *nice* party and it's going to get even *better,* and don't you worry about a *thing,* dahling!"

"But *sweet*heart," gushed Cash, showing her teeth in a grimace of a smile, "who's *wor*ried? *I'm* not worried. Are *you* worried?"

Arnold's leer drooped to a sneer and he looked her hard in the eye for a moment, then sat back and whispered something to Nancy-baby. And while he went on making soothing sounds on his side of her, Cash leaned in front of me and said into her other ear, "Honey, you look cold. Come inside and I'll dig out a sweater for you."

"Oh for gosh sakes!" said Nancy. "Let me finish eating, will you?"

We did, the two witchdoctors both poised with their conflicting spells, and me, snugly beside the patient.

12

WHEN SHE FINISHED EATING, she got up, walked to the garbage can behind the buffet table, dropped her paper plate in it, put her wooden bowl and fork on the table, turned and was immediately surrounded by Cash, who put both hands on her arm and marched her off to the girls' room.

"There," said Arnold. "See what she's doing? What in the world does the bitch think she's proving?"

"Which bitch?"

"Cash, you boob!"

"She's an angel of mercy," I muttered into my martini.

"She's a frustrated dyke," he shouted.

"There's something *wrong* here," I tried. "I don't like the *mood.*"

"Ha! Of course you don't! Look! Look what time it is —eight-fifteen. It's the first time we went past seven without breaking the ice, and it's all your fault, dunderhead."

"Maybe the ice is thicker."

"Thicker! Why, it's almost as thick as your head! If you'd only trusted me, done what I told you. Ah, but it's too late now. The damage is done. That vampire, she'll keep her in there all night—put her under lock and key, house arrest."

136

"Isn't there some other way? I mean does Nancy have to be the one? Can't they switch this year, get themselves a new girl?"

"Look, dunderhead, to all these other chicks there would be nothing more hum*ili*ating."

"I *realize* that, but why do they insist on humiliating Nancy-baby?"

"I told you, it's tradition!"

"But why can't they spread it around, enlarge the tradition?"

"Who knows?"

He threw up his arms in exasperation and began to walk away. Then he turned on me again: "Oh they'll *dream* it, these other chicks. They'll *be* Nancy vicariously—with every new guy she takes *on*. But *live* the dream—never! It's the same old story, dunderhead. Ah, I should have brought you here last year. Why didn't I? Oh yes, you were off to one of your silly swimming meets. But last year—whew! She was going up and down those stairs and in and out of that changing room all night long, and every time she went up with another one, you could *smell* it—these other bitties salivating—and it cracked the party wide open. After a while, anything went. Ah, well, it's just too bad things had to turn out this way this year. I was all set to see the party crack even wider open. Let it be a lesson to you, oaf. When your Uncle Arnie tells you to listen—*listen!*"

The electric guitars were on again and the dancing was resuming; it was as if the guests had given up hope that Nancy would take on the boys, now that she'd been sentenced to the girls' room, but the party would go on anyhow, despite this violation of hallowed tradition.

137

Then, about the time most of them were up and dancing, out came Cash with her captive; they went to Arnold and me, and Cash—as if she'd decided that dancing was just the thing to get everybody's mind off what had not happened—tugged us both to our feet and put Nancy into the care of Arnold, of all people, and took me for her own, and off we went to the middle of the patio to join the gyrating.

I was going halfheartedly through the motions and dreaming and scheming and rummaging through my mind, trying to find some way to make my soul-felt declaration to Nancy and get the two of us the hell out of all this. I figured that if the party could dance itself into a new mood—and already some of the flippant chatter was returning—I could switch partners with Arnold and get to Nancy-baby *some*how and get reestablished with her.

But this speculation was only a measure of how countrified dumb I was, for everyone was concentrating on his dancing now, oblivious to his partner's, and that should have been my first hint. And they were putting more snap into it than any of them had shown before. Between my scheming and this new crackling excitement the scene was jamming up and becoming, I even began to recover a little of what I'd lost—those juices of certain rebellions that would have this music move me—and I was beginning to receive these electrified sounds like it was rutting season at old Uncle Ned's early summer hoedown.

Then the record stopped and in the pause before the next one dropped, Mrs. what's-her-name, the caretaker's wife, appeared at Cash's side asking what she should do with the leftover hamburger meat. Cash told me she'd be right back, glanced around to check on Nancy and Arnold, and went with the woman into the kitchen.

The next record dropped and Arnold waved me over to come make a threesome, which took no coaxing. So here I was, in front of Nancy, whose fine head of dark hair was going all askew and jouncing to her dancing. And now her face was set with something like a new determination, and her eyes were wide and staring off into the darkness behind me. Arnold was keeping his attention on her like a hawk-eyed scientist on the subject of an experiment; his teeth were bared and gleaming in the colored lights, and he was dancing like a witchdoctor around a bedeviled patient. His voodoo was working too, for all of a sudden I realized that everyone was dancing with Nancy—either watching her directly or turning their dancing on her, like collectively casting a spell. And now the expression on her face was close to wretched and she was dancing up a storm, vibrating like she was having an orgasm with Almighty Creation, and some of the boys had left their partners and were moving in on her, turning their full attention and all their movements on her. Behind them, a few of the girls were sort of backing the boys in this, so our threesome had become a two-dozensome that was closing in, closing in on her. When the number ended it was one big tight mob around her and the kinky blond-haired chunky guy had somehow slipped through and was right up against her, elbowing me out of the way, and in the sudden silence between records he was running his hands lightly over her bare midsection and whispering into her ear.

I glanced around for Cash but all I could see was a swirl

139

of faces all peering into the middle of this mob scene and when I looked back, they were on their way—this chunky character had her by the hand and they were shoving their way out of that press, going quickly across the patio to the steps, down to the beach and into the darkness, toward the ocean.

And before the next record fell, another guy broke from the jam-up and went after them; and at the first sound of the new number, two more left, and after that a whole mob of guys—more than a dozen—went howling off down the steps to be swallowed up by the darkness.

Then I felt fingers kneading my biceps and Cash was back, muttering and moaning, "Oh no, oh no!"

Someone turned off the recordplayer then, for no one was dancing any more, and all we could hear was the pounding of the surf.

Cash said, "I just can't be*lieve* it!"

Arnold was on the other side of me, close to my ear, saying, "Well, what are *you* waiting for? This is *it,* dunderhead. Aren't you going?"

"No," I said. Regretfully.

"That's too bad. But then, it would be a bit messy down there, I suppose. Never happened this way before. Rather disappointing. However, looking at the broad picture, the way it's happening should have an interesting effect, later."

And I just stood there between them, with Arnold's voice in one ear and Cash's clutching fingers at my arm. I was feeling conflicting emotions and urges. I was sick about what was happening, yet I was even sicker about being left out of it all. The only other boys left out were Arnold, who didn't need it, and the male member of the

140

Lovers, and I was tempted to plead with them to help in some valiant effort to "save" Nancy. But that was a totally idiotic idea, for Arnold was delighted by what was happening and the Lover was sitting placidly beside his mate and they were looking like a couple of newlyweds waiting for a bus.

Then Cash made an announcement to the whole patio: "Isn't somebody going to *do* something?"

And when no one paid any attention to her, she shouted: "Doesn't anybody *care?*"

But the way those other bitches cared was something else. Cash was talking to herself.

The old caretaker was keeping strictly to his tasks, clearing the buffet table and cleaning up, and most of the girls —all but Judy—were clustered together near the seaside end of the patio with their collective gaze toward the beach, like so many grasswidows poised to hear news of the war. Except that they seemed vaguely satisfied, relieved, uplifted as they stood there stock still listening into the pounding surf, like waiting to relish any new sound that might take them closer to the rite.

Judy appeared from somewhere to stand on the other side of Cash, like offering herself as a sympathetic friend, but Cash was becoming more and more frantic.

"What are we," she yelled, "animals?"

And I couldn't help seeing, as I stood there looking around at them and waiting in this windless stillness, that there was being enacted here a scene just tailor-made for my poorboy's prejudice—these elegant sons and daughters of the rich and powerful demonstrating that they are just as cruel and rapacious as lowlier folk, and a whole lot more

141

snide about it into the bargain. And even though I was sickened by the fact that this prideful lust rite was taking as its victim the only one of them I had any affinity for, I was finding a grim satisfaction in it, and Cash's words "What are we, animals?" added to my satisfaction, for it made me ponder just what these elegants really were, compared to a pack of dogs after a bitch in heat. Dogs are much too honest to pull a trick like this—leave a dozen bitches in heat and go howling after only one. Why, these elegants were more like a pack of starving wolves after some sick or crippled creature—except that they were humans and the one they were after was their own kind and she was, likely as not, the healthiest one among them. For Cash to even suggest that they were animals was an insult to Creation. They were worse than animals—less than animals, more than animals. They were Yahoos.

It was too much. I heaved a sigh and bummed a cigarette from Arnold. Then the metallic taste of the smoke reminded me I hadn't eaten.

Cash, for the moment, was in a near-tearful conference with Judy, so I searched out a paper plate and went looking. The salad was gone but I found one forgotten hamburger, cold but better than nothing, and inside the door I located a package of buns, made my sandwich and began munching.

But as soon as I stepped back outside I was confiscated by Cash. She had me by the arm and was dragging me over to the seaside end, past the cluster of maidens in waiting and onto the first step down to the beach, like she was about to lead me to the lineup. Then she halted and stood there biting her lip and looking very pained. It seemed a phony pain and I was ignoring her the best I could, munching my hamburger and holding up a finger to feel the bare beginnings of a breeze starting to kick up again.

"You think it's funny?" she said angrily.

I wasn't going to get into a debate with my mouth full, but her tone tempted my oaf. I would have enjoyed agitating her put-on agony by saying something like, How *I* find this scene is *my* business, richbitch, so turn my arm loose and fuck off.

"Like I said," came Judy's voice from somewhere behind us, "this party is an undisputed flop."

Cash huffed, "Oh! Honestly!" Now she was mad at Judy too.

And then a gust of wind hit us, whipping the paper plate out of my hand and sending it skittering over the patio, and a few seconds later we were having a howling blow; things were being whisked off table tops and chairs were toppling, and the girls were clutching their disintegrating hairdos and the two caretakers were scurrying this way and that, trying to move things inside. Cash stood her ground, peering into the darkness with the wind lifting and tossing her hair.

I downed my last bite of hamburger just as the sun umbrella over one table flipped inside out; I was chewing, taking deep breaths and enjoying the feel of the strong wind on my face when I felt her pushing against my back. "Come on," she yelled into the wind as she tried to shove me down the steps, "we've just *got* to do *some*thing."

"Like *what?*"

"We've got to *stop* it. Oh! We *can* stop it, we've *got* to stop it!"

That conjured up a most distasteful scene in my mind:

143

her cheering me on from the sidelines while she had me taking on that pack of big beefy blustering elegants, half-gone on this celebration of their annual rite—me in the middle of that pack trying to keep them away from the sizzling meat they'd been sniffing all day long. Christ, I'd end up a basket case.

Then, as I took a deep breath to render my rebuttal to her absurd suggestion, lightning struck—over the ocean, lighting up the beach enough for us to glimpse the action: a huddled group of intent figures, like a crowd drawn to a fight.

Then came a loud crack of thunder that shook the steps we stood on, and before it had rumbled away the first of the pack appeared—the chunky blond guy, lumbering up through the sand out of the darkness, up the steps brushing past us, damp and sandy and wild-eyed. Cash spat at his back as he cantered over the patio toward the house.

And now the rain came—in big drops, making loud splats on the terrazzo, and wind-blown against our faces with stinging force. We were drenched in seconds and Cash was yelling, "My *things,* my *things!*"

Off she went at a brisk waddle and now I was alone with my face being scrubbed by the stinging drops, saying, "Yeah, yeah, oh yeah—your precious things. Go save your precious things." And I was also silently marveling at the timing old Mother Creation was showing, and beginning to get curious about just how Arnold was taking it all—his dessert being had on the beach and now this storm. Just where did this leave his masterplan?

Another of the pack ran by, this one almost knocking me off my feet, then I turned and walked slowly over the

144

slick patio as the pelting big raindrops fried on it. Everyone else had dashed inside and, in a way, it was a relief to be alone in this hard rain. Except that the way this party was going, it had me feeling like I'd felt that day at summer camp when I'd been given the choice between rowboats and canoes, had chosen both and gotten neither.

13

ON THE DRY SIDE of the sliding glass doors, four girls stood holding the big bowl of martini, looking for a place to put it down. A couple of other girls were round and about, scouting a place for it. Rainwater dripped into the martini from the holders wet-hanging hair and they had that impatient, slightly frantic expression, like moving men supporting a refrigerator while the boss broods over where it should go.

The recordplayer had been set down on the floor just inside the door and a couple of girls were on their hands and knees looking for an electrical plug-in. The lights from the aquarium were the only ones: the scene was surrounded by great canyons of darkness with globs of white in them.

Then some wall lights were turned on by Cash at a switch across the room near the front door; the girls with the bowl decided to give up and put it down on the floor beside the recordplayer, and the plug-in hunters found their socket. I spotted a wet towel on the floor near the door to the girls room and used it to wipe my face and hair; as I wiped, the guy who'd almost knocked me down on his return from the beach stood by calling for the towel; I took my time, then tossed it to him.

Girls were bemoaning the ruination of their hairdos,

146

sorting the wet records from the dry, and going into the girls' room to change into dry clothes; all during this, the doors kept rolling open to admit sheets of wind-driven rain and another returnee from the gangbang.

Now, with a dedication I found somewhat incomprehensible, the dancing got going again to the music blaring forth from the floor. The boys danced in soaked, sandy clothes; some of the girls who'd been soaked danced in their wet clothes instead of changing, and the ones who did change were being sprayed by the wet ones around them.

Well, their dancing was warming them, but I was shivering in my clothes and feeling very much the foreigner and considering the possibilities of stealing or borrowing some dry clothes. The only dry ones I had were in the trunk of the MG. But instead of going out into the rain again, I looked for Arnold—his dessert having been had on the beach, he might as well forget his silly masterplan and drive on to the mountains. So I was roaming around looking in the dark under jutting balconies, hoping to locate him back there where the cool colored lights of the aquarium and the frosted bare bulbs of the main room shed no illumination.

But I couldn't find him, and by now I was shivering furiously; I finally took off my shirt, pulled a sheet off a statue and dried my upper body, and this did me so much good I was tempted to crack the party further open by stripping down completely and drying off all over—when Cash came along.

"Oh, here you are," she said; we were on the kitchen-dining side of the aquarium, near the sliding glass doors; folded aluminum and wooden deck furniture had been

147

hastily moved in and put down here, and I had opened out one chair and was sitting in it.

She stood over me with her hands on her hips: "Randy, I need your help."

Well, at this point, she was saying exactly the wrong thing the wrong way, as far as I was concerned—like she was the queen and I was the stableboy and that request for help sounded like the kick-off for a long list of impossible orders. I ignored her, left her standing by waiting, went on rubbing myself down with the sheet. Then I got up, found a clean glass on the bar in the kitchen and went past her, past the aquarium to the bowl of martini and ladled myself out a glassful, hoping for some warmth from the alcohol. But here she was again, at my side, saying, *"Please! It's getting out of hand."*

"Well now, just what the hell do you want *me* to do about it? It's *your* party."

There was a second of looking her straight in the eye, seeing the dread that remark put into her. Then from somewhere across the big room, there came a loud shattering, a crash-tinkle, and she closed her eyes and said, "Oh my God!" And dashed off into the gloom to find out what had happened.

I'd nothing better to do, so I trailed along; someone had collided with a pedestal and knocked from the top of it a huge vase and it had shattered into hundreds of pieces. She was down on her haunches in the shadows hovering over it, lamenting it.

"Your precious things." I laughed to myself, and left her.

The truth of the matter was, the smashing of that vase

148

had given me some happy release inside, like the end of a long drought, and I walked away in a much better mood. Went rubbing the soles of my shoes rollingly over the sand on the floor as I went past the dancers. Wandering, shuffling aimlessly about, and was near the recordplayer when the music stopped in the middle of a number. Crouched over the recordplayer were a couple of girls with soaked clothes and hung-down hair—they hadn't liked the music that had been playing and were putting on a stack of their own selections—noisier, more electric guitars, more insistent drums. When they stood up again, one of them paused long enough to look me up and down in a harsh, deadpanned way I could only suppose was meant to be flirtatious, but struck me like the look of an angry housewife shopping for meat. Still, it was the most direct and overt sign any of them had shown toward the fact of my existence, aside from formal introductions, and I was tempted to bow from the waist. All I did, though, was stare at her bra—her thin blouse was clinging to her padded bra, showing those tiny ripples in the fabric, as she stood there looking me over with her face flushed from the exertions of dance—so I stared at her padded bra, until she turned back to the dance and joined in again.

There were about twice as many girls dancing as guys, but returnees from the gangbang were still popping in with regularity and, after short rubdowns with wet towels, joining in. About every minute or so the glass doors would roll open and send in angry slashes of wind-driven rain accompanied by a drenched and sandy elegant, who'd shove the door shut, mop his face, and beaming triumph and strutting proud, go into the thick of the dance.

149

The quality of which now was something else—as if the girls had taken off the invisible girdles of their earlier movements and the guys had been made more loose of limb by their release of gism; and it seemed to me, as I stood against a wall and watched them, that they were, for a certain, celebrating the gangbang. And maybe the rainstorm too, since both had made significant contributions to the present mood of the party. A few of the girls now looked for all the world like they were—just as Arnold had suggested—pretending to be Nancy-baby: they were dancing with that certain vibrant tension she'd shown, shaking their hair about and gazing vacantly off into patches of darkness. Some of the boys were now clowning and improvising variations that were expressive, that told about their dreamlives, and there was a definite undercurrent of desperation in it now, as if just beneath the surface of this celebration of their annual rite lurked a more murderous lust.

I stood watching this celebration, thinking back to a time in the orphanage when, on one crisp night in fall with a full and urgent moon out, a gang of us kidnapped a boy from his bed and took him, tied and gagged, out of the dorm and down the fire escape, down a manhole into a tunnel that ran under the building—he was a scholarly fellow who had somehow gotten the reputation of taking it in the mouth, but closer to the truth of our motive, our attack, was his manner of speaking, dressing, acting, which we considered "aristocratic and uppity," by which we meant pretentious—so down there in the tunnel we forced him to take all of us, took turns holding him on his knees with his hands behind his back, and using him. But when it was

150

all over and we let him up and he walked silently away, climbing the ladder up out of the manhole and the fire escape steps to the dorm, we followed quietly, unlike this celebration here before me.

By now, all the celebrants were back from the beach and the middle of the main room's floor was a free-swinging jam session of shaking hips, flying arms and moving feet on that floor that had been made slick by sand. The sight of Cash elbowing her way through this jam brought me out of my trance-like staring; she was solemnly carrying pieces of the broken vase toward the kitchen, where she dropped them in a wastepaper basket and got a dustpan and broom from the closet, and went to get the rest. The dancers never noticed her; they'd been completely captured by the rhythms and their joys of celebration.

I was feeling sick and depressed by it all when I walked out to the foot of the stairway with tentative plans to wander up to the second floor and look for Arnold, for neither Harry nor Mary, I'd noticed, were out on the floor now—they'd gone off somewhere after Harry's return from the gangbang. Then, at the foot of the stairs, I paused to undrape the empty suit of knight's armor there; I figured to make my own addition to the scene, my comment, with this empty undraped presence my emissary. So I flung off the sheet, tossed it away and bowed elegantly, saluted him with my martini before going wearily up the steps. About halfway up, I glanced back down to inspect the effect the guardianship of my emissary was having on the rhythmic writhing of the celebrants—which he was, sure enough, viewing most grandly, his trusty sword held poised—when

151

the sliding glass doors rolled open once more, sending in wind and rain, and this time into the room gingerly stepped the cause of the celebration.

Immediately there was a lull in the dancing, like someone was to make an important announcement and they were cocking half an ear; they slowed their dancing to a near stop and were turning toward her while the music blasted on insistently. She was wearing a brown sweater which one of the boys had been wearing, and it took both her hands to hold it down front and back over her bare bottom. Rainwater poured from her onto the floor as, keeping both hands on ends of the sweater, she leaned against the door and pushed it closed with her body. There were patches of sand on the backs of her thighs just beneath the sweater's bottom; my attention went to these patches and I got lost in trying to visualize how the overhang of her butt had sheltered this sand from the driving downpour. Maybe she'd been trying to sneak in unnoticed— there was a hint of cringing shyness in her posture, her knees slightly bent, her head down, her face almost hidden between shades of wet hair that hung down both sides of her face—but when she realized she was, again, the center of their hot attention—for by now the dancing had come to a complete standstill—she straightened her back and lifted her face to them, and it was a moment I'll not soon forget.

For if they had made her their humiliated victim, the receptacle of their own self-loathing, had collectively shot into her some nasty disgrace which had threatened their pretentious elegance, were now rid of it and turning to

152

inspect her to see how well she was managing to carry this burden of nasty disgrace—Nancy, by the way she met their inspecting eyes, shot their nasty disgrace right back at them, rejected. She looked hard at each of them, one by one, and one by one they turned away and tried, self-consciously at first, to resume dancing and to attract their partners back to the dance. Soon Nancy was staring at dancers who were glancing sheepishly at her out of the corners of their eyes, and she had stared them down.

I sat down on a step; I was tempted to applaud.

Finally, Nancy lowered her face, turned to the stairs and was coming up toward me slowly, her face sagging, losing the fierce show of defiance which had buttressed it a moment ago, and she was mumbling something. It wasn't until she had reached me and was on her way past me that I heard, over the loud music, what she was saying: "My clothes . . . what did they do with my clothes?"

God only knows what they did with her clothes—threw them into the surf, most likely. I guided her to the top of the stairs and stationed her back in a shadowy corner there; then I went down the stairs two at a time, around into the girls room, turned on all the lights and began to hunt.

I relished the task, made the place fly—panties, bras, blouses, shorts and a variety of slacks went sailing hither and yon out of overnight bags and into the general tangled mess of wet towels, rejected. I made it a point to reject everything in every bag before I finally found a nice clean pair of panties, an expensive-looking blouse with a loud red-and-white print, and a pair of Capri pants she could squeeze into. I went about tossing bras up in the air for a while, then decided I'd not insult her healthy tits with any sag-supporter worn by any of these elegants—I'd not chance the spread of some as yet undiscovered disease.

Then I carried my catch through the curious gaze of the celebrants and up the stairs I went, finding their hostile attention inspiring; halfway up, I paused to get all the clothes in one hand so I could pick up my drink, then I cast down upon their upturned faces my most countrified, and continued on to the top of the stairs where she was waiting in the shadow with her teeth chattering and her body wretched with the shivers. I put an arm around her and guided her down the long, dark hallway, past the boys' room to hunt for a room she'd be sure to have all to herself. In the first room we came to were the Lovers, in the second were Vikie, Vallery and a boy, a new petitioner for Vikie's flirtations being bugged by Vallery's interference. We went all the way to the room Cash had taken me into, explored its darkness with "Hellos" and gropings and found it empty, so it became hers. But she paused just inside the door and waited; I dropped her clothes on the bed and said, "Here, Nancy, sit down over here, I put your clothes here."

She made a high-pitched pup-like sound I took to mean, "Yes," but she didn't move; she stayed hovering against the wall, battling her shivers, and, I guessed from the pitch of her voice, trying to hold back tears.

"Here's some sheets you can dry off with," I tried, but she kept tight to the wall. Then it dawned on me—she's afraid I'm going to take up the end of the line!

The thought gave me a jolt and I made haste to get out of the room and leave her alone. I walked slowly back the dark hallway, sipping my martini, pausing to marvel at the varieties of sounds that were coming to me—the music and dancing from below and now some clomp-clomping from above, someone in the third-floor hallway. Well, Arnold, Harry and Mary were the only ones I hadn't seen someplace recently, so I began looking for a way up. But whatever stairway I'd used to get there earlier was nowhere to be found at the moment, so I gave up looking and took to diverting myself by pulling the sheets off things along the hallway and inspecting them again, and this amusement carried me to a spot I liked—where one wall of the hall ended and the hallway turned into a balcony opening onto the doings down below. I slung a leg over the banister and rested my back against the wall's end; it seemed like a fine place to sip and contemplate their activities; it provided me enough darkness to give a feeling of privacy I found comfortable. Then too, here I could keep an eye out for the sight of Arnold—maybe he'd pop out onto one of those balconies across the way.

I was squinting into the dimness of those far-off balconies when he scared me so bad I panicked over tumbling down to the main floor—suddenly, out of nowhere, he was at my shoulder, tapping and asking, "Have you seen them?"

"Seen who?" I blurted, banging both feet down onto the floor of the hallway.

"My main course and dessert."

I felt like my knees would buckle. "Jesus! Give it up, will you?"

"No, I won't give it up, dammit." He touched the rim of my glass with the rim of his and said, "The party's just getting started."

"Man, your dessert was *had*—on the beach. He made that scene *too,* you know."

"Yes, very uncouth of him, wasn't it."

"Look," I pleaded, "let's go on to the mountains—this party's a big, loud, wet nothing! And those two—*they* don't want *you!* Isn't that *clear* by now?"

He turned away and went walking off. "How do they know *what* they want?"

That stopped me for a second; then, as an afterthought, I hollered, "How does the grass know to be green?"

But that brought nothing back from him; he prowled on through the dark of the hall.

I went back to my perch on the banister moping over what a grim, gory, forced march through the Russian winter was his put-on faggotry, what an idiotic situation it had gotten us both into here, and wondering for the umpteenth time how a guy who had everything could *be* that way. Why, if I looked anything like a tall, dark Arab chieftain, I'd . . .

I began to feel like I did the time I lost my first race—tired and unconcerned, too weary to care any more.

That happened one cold, bleak Saturday afternoon at West Point when—

But there's no need to go into that. Besides, it's something I'd rather forget.

14

A FEW MORE SIPS and I'd drained my glass, so I went for a refill.

When I reached the foot of the stairs and was giving a salute to my knight, some chick turned on me, dancing to me, like inviting me into the jam. It was one of the pair who'd said what anywoman wanted, the two I'd presented with the essence of my manhood and . . . I had a quick flick of temptation to drop my glass to the floor and join her—it was Chuck Berry's "Roll Over Beethoven" they were on, and that, after all, was my music. Or had been before it got taken over by those who fuck with fickle fashion. And now it had this daughter of them dancing like an Indian brave priming for battle—but I didn't feel up to coping with what kind of a anywoman that was.

It was this last thought that doused cold water on my temptation. Sent me off muttering to myself that surely we have-nots have already handed those haves more than they ever bargained for and they were flirting with disaster when they confiscated our music this way—as a means of getting themselves temporarily out of their straitjackets of propriety, which they'd only put on again after this celebration was over and wear to lord themselves over me

157

and my kind once more. Besides, they make war so much better than they dance.

So onto the elegant, crystal, floored bowl of booze I went, putting my back to her invitation; this time I didn't bother with the silver ladle but used my glass as a dipper, then went my lonely way back upstairs. I roamed to my right on the second-floor landing and found that by going around to about three-quarters of a full circle and into an alcove, I came to the stairway up to the third floor. I took it, groping slowly and carefully through the pitch-black darkness, and emerged to overlook the goings-on below from a balcony up there. I paused here long enough to note a new development: a couple of boys with Judy girl clown trying to figure out a way to get her into the empty suit of knight's armor, the one I'd de-sheeted and set on them as my comment. This little group had taken my knight and slipped off from the dancing, and were on the far side of the stairway, between the stairs and the girls room, and they were diligently trying to dismantle the knight and make him accommodate Judy.

I would have remained with this spectacle longer if it looked like the success of their project was possible, but my knight was well put together and they weren't making much headway, so I roamed on.

Down the hall I went with my fingers sliding along the wall to my left, knocking things over occasionally, until I came to an opening and, after some groping, found that it took me to the far side of the main room, to the third-floor balcony over there.

Earlier in the day I'd traveled this connecting hallway when I was coming down from the lookout nest, but I hadn't managed to find the stairway I'd just come up then —the house was that sort of a maze.

Well, I was having a sip of martini to mark my progress when I heard the tinkle of a girl's giggle from a nearby room. I felt my way to the nearest door and pushed it open. Back in its innards there was a dim ray of light; I went to it and found a door to a bathroom. It, in turn, connected with another room and that's where the light was coming from. Also voices, two of them—male and female. Their door to the bathroom was partly open; I sat down on a broad windowsill in the bathroom and became a peeping Tom on the doings of Mary and Harry.

Mary was wearing a plumed hat—a Victorian-looking thing with a long, fluffy white feather hung down the side of it—a relic she'd dug up and was prizing. She was standing in front of a mirror, above which was a bare bulb; Harry was behind her with his arms boldly around her waist and they were laughing at the image of the be-hatted Mary in the mirror. She was making faces at herself, turning her head this way and that. They chattered away for a while, getting along famously now. Then Harry said, "Wasn't that a bathroom we passed?"

I left my perch ready to flee.

"Yes," said Mary, "two doors down the hall."

"Be right back," he said, and walked out the door to the hallway, leaving her alone.

She went on making faces and clowning into the mirror —until, suddenly, she drew in her breath with a frightened "*Uh!*" And disappeared from my sight in a confusion of loud rustling sounds.

She was on the bed now—I got that from the sort of

159

rustling I was hearing. But I was also hearing more sinister sounds, like a grunting, thrashing struggle.

To find out what the hell was going on, I had to poke my head around the door between us—and there on the sheet-covered, canopy-topped bed it was: the blue-and-white-striped polo shirt of Arnold bouncing about and being heaved back and forth as he tried to hold Mary pinned down and she struggled for all she was worth.

I was drawn all the way into the room by this; I wasn't sure I was seeing what I was seeing. I guess Arnold had been hiding somewhere out in the hall, and when Harry left, he slipped in, clapped a hand over her mouth, tossed her down on the bed, and here they were. He was trying to stuff a corner of the bed's sheeting into her mouth with one hand, and she was twisting and thrashing and trying to get out a good loud scream. With the other hand, he was working to pry her legs apart, at the same time trying to keep her down with the weight of his body.

Well, the speed and surprise of this scene had me standing there stock still, hang-jawed, non-plused. I'd just set my glass down and was about to come pouncing to the maiden's rescue when who should materialize out of the darkness but Harry, back from taking a leak. He gawked at the scene for a second, then rushed over and grabbed Arnold by the shoulders and pulled him with a mighty grunt off the bed and onto the floor. Then, while Arnold sat there laughing and shoving his wang back into his pants, Harry said to Mary, "You okay?"

She let out a cry of relief and they patted each other tenderly for a while—long enough for Arnold to slide backward over the floor toward the door to the hall, and as soon as Harry left the bedside to deal with his faggot-cum-foe, Arnold scrambled to his feet and cut out, with Harry close on his heels bellowing with rage, and the two of them went pounding away down the hall.

Balancing my martini carefully, I shuffled along after them, giving Mary one more fright as I went by—appearing out of nowhere, to her, a few feet away. From down the hall came the sounds of thumping feet and falling objects, and as I went, I found tables had been shoved out into the middle of the hall, their contents spilled to the floor, and display racks had been ripped down from walls—Arnold doing the best he could to obstruct Harry's path.

The hall led to a stairway, and near the top of it I found Harry, panting and practically glowing with rage. But not going down into the darkness of this enclosed stairway.

"Hey! What's going on?" I said.

He swung around and shoved past me and went cursing and fumbling back through the hall. I was sure he wasn't giving up the chase, so he must be looking for another way downstairs to intercept Arnold.

I decided to go down these stairs. I listened intently into the darkness for Arnold but all I could hear was my own breathing. I was making my way gingerly down when I stepped on something round and it rolled under my foot and sent me almost tumbling. Another path-obstructing object Arnold had left in his wake. I kept my feet but the near fall spilled my drink—up, out of the glass and down wetly over me. I took time out to swab my hair and wipe

161

my face, then I set the empty glass down on a step and went on with both hands working the walls and made it down to the second floor.

Here I gave up the chase; I was on a balcony with a fine view. It overlooked the huge aquarium—the balcony floor was almost flush with the top of the tank, which was about three feet wide; by looking over the railing you could see right down into the weedy, fishy water. The lights from it were directed out onto the main-room floor, where the dancing was still in high gear, most of it directly in front of the aquarium, so that I could crouch on my haunches like a weary dirtfarmer up here above the water and watch the doings, as if from the dark side of the moon, and this appealed to me.

I checked the scene: the dancing and the progress of the project to put Judy into the knight's armor. Cash was going around down there trying diplomatically to button-hole this one and that one for brief consultations. Which ended—the few I watched—with the buttonholed breaking free and going back to the dancing. She was still bugging everybody to be careful of the things, her father's precious things.

Well, I decided to roam on, and this time as I made my way into the dark innards of the house I kept track of my route so I could get back to that spot above the aquarium. Down the hall I was into now, tables were still in place against the walls, display racks still hanging and all was correctly covered with sheet. I went all the way to the end of this hall, opening doors and shouting into rooms: "Arnold!" I thought if I did run across him, he'd be ready to split for the mountains now, but I didn't find him.

162

Then the hall came to a deadend at a door with light peeping out the cracks around it, and from the other side of this door I heard voices in animated chatter—then music. I pressed my ear to it and the mystery was dispersed by the bleating of a TV commercial. I figured some of the partiers were watching TV, so I tried to turn the door and go in, but it was locked. Then I bent and looked through the keyhole and bobbing back and forth across my line of vision was the caretaker woman in a rocking chair. I silently begged her pardon and departed.

I was on my way back through the hall toward the light from the top of the balcony over the aquarium, when—coming toward me with their backs to this light appeared a trio of explorers, two girls and a boy. I stopped and watched. It was, I learned from their voices, Vikie, Vallery and their latest boy, and they were wandering through the place with Vikie making cute flirtatious remarks to the boy and Vallery, like her superego, still driving her inane chatter between them like a wedge, and the boy having not much to say but plotting, no doubt, to have things his way eventually, somehow.

Suddenly two of them disappeared. Vallery was alone, talking on. After a moment of that, she swung around, looked this way and that and realized she'd been deserted.

She stalked back to the last door they'd passed and began pounding on it, calling, "Vikie, Vikie! Are you in there, Vikie?"

"Yes, we're in here," came Vikie from the other side.

"Well, what's up?"

"Nothing. But we can't get the door open."

"Can't get the door open!"

"No! Does it open from your side?"

Sounds of giggles came from the far side of the door.

"Vikie, what are you *doing*?"

"*Noth*ing, honey, just trying to get this silly *door* to open."

"It doesn't open from *my* side."

"Well, *try*."

"I *am* trying," moaned the struggling Vallery as she wrestled with the doorknob.

"It *must* open from your side," insisted Vikie, saying "must" like the boy had just goosed her.

Vallery kicked the door and yelled, "Oh, Vikie! I'm *mad* at you!"

"Why?" came Vikie with a squeal of delight.

"Come on *out* of there."

"I can't, I told you, this silly door won't open."

More giggling from the room.

"Oh, Vikie, you're just . . . you're just . . ."

"Are you *try*ing to open it?"

Vallery was leaning her back against it now, standing with her arms folded over her bosom, huffing and puffing with hurt and anger.

"Vallery . . . ?"

She didn't answer. She brushed a hand over her face, then moved away into the center of the hall, smoothed down her skirt and went with short, quick, determined steps away.

"Vallery? Are you there, Vallery?"

Then the boy said something I couldn't hear, and after that Vikie's tone changed. "Vallery, don't *leave* me here! For gosh *sakes!* . . .

164

"Vallery, where *are* you? . . .

"*Say!* Now you just stop that sort of thing! Don't *do* that. Jim! I'm *asking* you, *please!* . . .

"Vallery! Come *back* here!"

Then the door flew open and out dashed Vikie with the end of her blouse hanging over the waist of her skirt; she cut to her right like a halfback and went scampering down the hall and disappeared around the bend. Jim followed at a slow walk, tucking in his shirttail and muttering to himself.

I gave him time to be well on his way, then I went back to my place above the aquarium; I found I now shared it with the four-legged Diogenes, who was sitting there on his haunches, surveying the party below through the uprights of the railing. His attitude seemed that of an aging monarch gazing down from his throne onto the heads of guests at a masquerade ball, cocking his head to one side, then the other, like trying to guess which guests were wearing which costumes.

Or, maybe in the case of this particular Diogenes, he was searching, with his lantern eyes, for a *practical* one among these sons and daughters of the rich and powerful, some one of them practical enough to declare his need graciously and gain satisfaction in a good and honest way. For clearly their need was to fuck, and it was just as clear that a gentle, goodhearted, orderly approach to dealing with this need was outside their sense of the possible. To take turns using Nancy-baby's body to jackoff into was acceptable enough, as long as it was done in a dramatic, vicious, humiliating way and not with such sweetness and gentleness it would elevate her social standing by acknowl-

165

edging what she was—the one most desired—and take into account her own needs—she being nothing if not anxious to please—instead of insulting her by acting like vultures—pecking awhile, then flying off to make way for the next pecker—never giving her even the satisfaction of gauging her own power to please. Well, it pleased me to imagine that in some remote place in his cat's subconscious, the redoubtable Diogenes knew of all of this. And when, as I stood by him, he took time out from his gazing down at the party to glance up at me, it pleased me to imagine I was in the company of a wise and very practical four-legged guru.

It was about this time that the sight of some tippling activity around the floored booze bowl caught my eye and reminded me that I had dumped my own drink onto my head coming down the stairs, and I departed Diogenes' company temporarily to go fetch me another. Around to my left I found a stairway that took me down to the kitchen; I went around the aquarium, past the dancers, who seemed now to be winding down from the more frenzied spirit they'd shown fresh in wet from the gangbang. I hunted up a glass, dumped the dregs of someone's last drink from it onto the floor, and waited my turn at the booze bowl.

A few feet away, the project to get Judy into the knight's armor was still in progress; it had, in fact, attracted a few more of them and a noisy argument was on over how to separate the knight's legs from his torso, and whether or not it was necessary to the project to do this. Some boys were doing the arguing; Judy didn't care one way or the other, and she was hoisting her glass now and then to punctuate someone's point with "Yeah!" The knight, meanwhile—that empty gone one I had so deftly set over them as my commentary on their doings—was flat on his back with his helmet off and his limbs near disjointure. I kept expecting Cash to arrive any moment, and wondering why she'd not come to the rescue of this gallant figure they were twisting their brains to dismantle, but she was nowhere to be seen.

The group around the booze bowl was trying to spoon out some cigarette ashes that had dropped into the martini. No telling how long that would take; I became impatient and reached an arm between the shanks of a couple and dipped my glass full, which brought a few astounded stares.

Then I departed their elegant company and was going through the kitchen toward the stairs when, right beside me, the phone rang. Now ringing phones always have made me nervous—I never knew what telephones were all about, quite, till I was twelve and got put in that orphanage—so this ring-a-ding here had me doing sort of buck-and-a-wing step. I kept trying to make myself go on to the stairs and forget it, but every time that mothah gave another ring I'd halt and do a doublestep, spilling martini on the floor.

My dilemma was strikingly ended when a strident female voice screeched:

"Don't touch that!"

And Cash emerged from the stairway waving her arms at me like I was chickens she was shooing. She went quickly to the phone and hovered over it, guarding it. "It's my father—if he hears this racket he'll skin me alive."

"The party is getting rough, isn't it."

She turned wide, angry eyes on me: "Have you *seen* the upstairs? Or did you *do* it?"

"Do what?"

"What!" she said, lowering her face as if the question were too absurd to even consider. Then, as an afterthought, she sneered, "Why don't you be the *first* to leave."

"I can't. Have to wait for Arnold. We're going to the mountains."

"Huh! Arnold! You'll find him on the second-floor balcony outside. He's out there with a *rope*. I don't know what he intends to do with it. Hang himself, I hope."

I moved to go there.

"And when you see him," she added, "tell him thanks. Thanks for everything."

I left her hovering over the ringing telephone and went up the stairs two at a time and began hunting for a way to the outside balcony. I had managed to get there on my afternoon trip through the house, but I couldn't remember which room I'd gone into to get there from. And the rooms were so pitch dark now, it took me a while to find the right room and make it.

Outside the rain had stopped but the wind was ferocious. I looked to right and left along the long balcony, but saw no one. I called softly into the wind, "Arnold . . . ?"

No answer.

So I cupped my hands around my lips against the wind and hollered to right, then left, and out of the deep shadows he stepped.

He waved for me to come on over. He was, sure enough, holding a rope. Had it looped up into a lasso.

168

"Listen," he said, "do me a favor, dunderhead. Go find that dear boy and tell him I'm out here."

"What the hell do you plan to do?"

"Catch him! Tie him up! Put a gag in his stupid mouth and talk some sense into him."

I leaned against the wall and took a sip from the glass before I attempted to come-back on that.

"Arnold, wait a minute. Now what kind of a tactic is this?"

"I'm tired of tactics. Brute force, that's all this one understands, so brute force it is. I'll overcome him."

"For crissakes, Arnie, you need that shrink again. Come on, let's get out of here—this party's about to make us *both* sick."

"Oh no! We'll stick around. You don't know these parties like I do. It'll liven up, you'll see."

Liven up!

"There's nothing *here* for us. Let that pair go and forget it and let's move on."

"Okay," he said, "but first, you find him and tell him where I *am,* and then we'll be ready to leave."

"Oh Christ!"

I walked away from him and he called after me: "Just tell him where I am, that's all."

"I ain't tellin' nobody nothin'."

He came after me carrying his stupid lasso hanging coiled in his hand. "Listen, you *must* do that for me, you *must. Every*thing depends on it."

"Yeah, okay," I said, to get away from him.

I went in through the room and back down the hall to

169

my balcony, my place by the regal Diogenes, and I squatted down on my haunches beside him, and here we were, peering at the party from between the carved wooden uprights of the banister.

My soaked clothes had been giving me trouble, galling my crotch and generally making me chilly and miserable, and when I spotted an abandoned beach towel on our balcony, it gave me an idea. I stripped everything off but my shoes and socks and hung them here and there to dry, and I wrapped up Indian fashion in the beach towel, which improved my lot considerably.

As I was settling myself again on my haunches beside the austere Diogenes, I saw that the project to put Judy into the knight's armor had overcome its impasse and was moving briskly toward completion; she was stepping—with much pretended balking at the idea of it—her legs into the knight's, and a gang of boys, rocking back and forth with laughter, were holding the knight's torso in readiness. Judy made it, finally, into the legs, then she struggled like one being put to torture as they lowered his torso over hers; her arms made it into the sleeves and they moved, then her head emerged through the top of the torso and there were cheers all around. They kept trying to give the sword to her but her hands, it seemed, didn't reach into the knight's mail gloves and the sword kept falling to the floor. Eventually they gave up with the sword and clapped the helmet down over her head and there she was, standing there with the others prancing around, lifting the visor to look in, having it fall down and lifting it again. A couple of guys were laughing so hard they could hardly stand up.

Then Judy made her move, and it was not without dramatic impact. Out into the midst of the dancers she went like some kind of a zombie from a time-machine movie, with her accomplices trailing their walking creation. The dancing stopped, the music wailed on and now the party revolved around Judy girl knight; everyone got to look inside the visor and see that, sure enough, you guessed it —Judy! Everyone got a kick out of this. Judy was making a valiant effort to put her knighthood to the movements of the dance, but these movements were really not the sort he could perform with anything approaching the style of the times. Even so, Sir Judy got a host of partners and loud encouragement for her efforts.

I was absorbed in this spectacle when, from behind me, Arnold said, "Great friend you are!"

And I turned just in time to see him disappear around the bend and into the stairway down to the kitchen. I scanned the balconies facing mine for signs of the hunter, then, and I wondered if I should be getting back into my wet clothes, ready for a hasty retreat. If Harry does find him, I'll wind up either stranded here or driving that MG to the nearest hospital. But Harry was nowhere to be seen and the thought of getting back into those wet clothes was too much, so I stayed put to await developments.

Someone had brought in a ladder with hooks on one end and was hooking it over the top rim of the aquarium, and then he was climbing up it toward us, me and Diogenes. It was the guy with the dark hair falling over his forehead, the erstwhile classics fan, and there was glee in his open-mouthed smile.

Up the ladder he came and down into the tank went his arm, like a spear. He was gone fishin'. He never even

171

noticed us two who observed his activities from about four feet away; he went right to work jabbing his arm down into the water, grabbing at this fish and that, sending all the inhabitants of the tank into frantic divings and dashings, and causing the seaweed to wave and shimmy. I saw him glance slyly to one side, trying to measure the attention he was getting, and I felt like telling him—he was indeed giving Sir Judy a run for the money, especially with some of the boys. I guess they'd worked so hard on the project of her knighthood they were ripe for this diversion he was offering, for they began to whoop it up for him.

Which proved too inspiring. The fisherman first went up one more rung so he could get his arm deeper into the water, then he went up another rung, and then he plunged his arm so deep and with such determination after one big fish that he, himself, went into the tank—his ambition had lost him his balance and over the rim he went and, having gone that far, splashed on in.

So there he was in the water now, the undisputed attention-getter, upstaging Sir Judy so well she was left struggling to lift her visor so she could see what the new fuss was all about.

On the outside of the glass, a lineup of fans urged the diver on with shouts and arm-wavings, and under the water he grabbed this way and that after any and all fish anywhere near him. It was thirsty work; he was soon in need of air, and he came up on a modified scissor kick that bumped the tank's glass casing. He panted awhile and listened to the cheers and acclaim offered by those below. Then—not to be satisfied with anything less than a catch

172

—he did a neat surface dive and down he went for another try.

This time he went much deeper, determined to fish the bottom, where most of his prey had gone to get away from him; the tank was about twelve feet deep and he made it to the bottom in great style and was prowling about down there, stirring up big clouds of silt, when—from above these clouds of silt—came waves of disturbance that brought me to my feet. I leaned out over the banister to peer down for a better look; from below, in the crowd, came the sound of Cash's voice, mingling with the others—she was yelling something I couldn't hear in the general din of screaming and shouting.

Through the thick clouds of silt I could barely make out what was going on—the fisherman had gotten tangled up in seaweed and was trapped down there. His frantic struggle to free himself was causing hefty undulations all the way up on the surface.

I tossed off my beach towel and was about to go diving to the rescue when I realized I'd be performing this operation in the nude. Which made me pause and ponder whether I should slip on my underwear shorts. I had decided to hell with it, I'd just dive in as was when the urgent need for action on my part was abated by the appearance of another. A lifeguard was coming up the ladder fully clothed. A stalwart fellow with weightlifter's biceps and a strong jaw. Over the top he went and down into the murky depths. I put my towel back around me and settled down to watch.

Which I was in the wrong place to do; those below on the outside of the tank had a much better view of it. Mine

173

was hopelessly obstructed now by the great clouds of silt, so I watched the faces of those below as they stared into the tank; they were intent, a few with the leftovers of smiles, a couple of girls with hands clapped over their mouths, most of them stern, silent, tense.

Suddenly into the crowd came Arnold. He appeared from the kitchen side of the aquarium, stepped into their midst and made himself conspicuous by putting his back to the tank and staring about with his legs bent and arms out like a base runner about to steal second. Or a cornered animal. Anyway, he moved cautiously to his left through the crowd and headed for the front door with his back to the glass and the others were so zeroed in on the rescue operation they paid no attention to him.

He reached the outer end of the tank and then from across the way, on the balcony facing mine near the top of the main stairway—there was Harry; he had taken a lance down from the wall display and was hefting it like a javelin—he was rearing back and letting fly with it—and here it came, looking like it was going to put an end to me! I hugged the floor and was ready to dodge, watching its final trajectory—down, and with a mighty and nightmarish crash, into the glass side of the aquarium.

15

Even the serene Diogenes was disturbed. He was the first one I saw when I opened my eyes after the shattering crashes and booming roar of escaping water had died to a tinkle and a trickle; there he was, backed off in the shadow of the hallway, hissing and crouched as though to leap. Well, I was the only one around for him to leap at, so I kept an eye on him for a while and talked to him till he quit his hissing.

Then I looked over my balcony and down, and was having myself a bird's-eye view of the damage. The steel frame of the aquarium was naked now and big chunks of broken glass lay on the floor under silty water and seaweed. And fish—big fish, little fish, all flipping and flopping in and out of forests of seaweed and over the floor, on the stairs, everywhere. And standing around this incredible puddle were the wide-eyed, horrified, deeply perplexed elegants—they were staring at it, this gigantic mess of slimy water, floating seaweed, flopping fish, big pieces of jagged glass, like disbelieving that this horrendous event had actually happened. None seemed to know what caused it—I guess it seemed to them like the tank had just collapsed at them in a series of loud crumples and crashes, for Harry's lance had hit the glass above and to the right

175

of where they'd been clustered, at the end nearest the patio. They'd scattered as the tank buckled—had fled the big chunks of plate glass that now lay cracked and shattered on the floor, right where the celebration had been.

Under which lay Judy, and now a gang of them ran to the rescue. Sir Judy was sprawled in her armor under the weight of a large piece of glass that had stayed intact; three or four of them went wading into this weedy, fishy, writhing puddle and they carefully lifted the glass and dragged the be-knighted Judy out from under it and onto the outer edge of the puddle. They propped her hapless armored figure against the wall and pulled off her knight's head to confront a gagging, drenched and slightly hysterical girl clown.

And as that was going on, the two swimmers were coming to life with some slushing and scratching sounds. I leaned out over my balcony to see what had become of them—they were prone on the bottom of the empty tank with a large piece of plate glass over them like half a pitched roof. It had dropped unbroken and got lodged at an angle and had protected them from the jagged ends of other chunks of falling glass which could have knifed right through them.

Now their roof of glass was lifted and they were carefully extracted from the wet ooze—first the burly lifeguard, who lay on top of the fisherman, and then the fisherman, who emerged with globs of muddy silt plopping from him, seaweed clinging to him, coughing and violently retching in a hoarse voice.

Judy was out of her armor now and getting shakily to her feet, trying out her legs in a short, rubbery stroll, and the others were wandering around inspecting themselves

176

and each other. When the lance hit, it must have caused the water to erupt mightily and go shooting out of the tank, for strands of seaweed had been flung great distances and a couple of little fish were halfway up the main stairway, flopping silently on its nice carpeting. The sheet over the medieval horse dressed for the tilting contest was drenched and the glass doors to the patio had silty water streaking down them. Girls were tugging at wet blouses and one was taking hers off and walking around in her bra, and the guys were pulling off their shirts and shaking them to get rid of the silt and weed. But as far as I could tell, everybody was okay, nobody seriously hurt. The worst case being the fisherman, and he was still lying on the floor retching and gagging, attended by three others.

Both Harry and Arnold had disappeared; Cash was on her knees beside the stairway with her hands over her face, rocking back and forth in mourning. Which got interrupted by another crash—some guy'd been sloshing through the puddle and knocked over a bust from the top of a podium and it hit a chunk of glass to shatter a spiderweb design.

And all during this the recordplayer blared on. Like our illustrious species' fatal fascination with things that go boom could have the world coming to an end but that mechanical motherfucker would have cared not at all—it had its tune to get through and by golly it did. And then the scene was put into a sudden, eerie silence, punctuated by the fisherman's gagging. Everybody was just standing around looking lost and dazed when, from somewhere in the bowels of the house, came a short, loud shriek. *"Ha!"* Like a laugh. Then there was a resounding WHUMP! And there in the middle of the floor lay this statue, broken into about a dozen

177

chunky pieces. Then there was the sound of malicious female laughter coming from somewhere and everybody was looking around for the source of it. Way up on the third floor, hanging over the railing of a balcony, was a girl, and she was wearing the red-and-white print blouse I'd found for her—Nancy. Down on the main floor, the elegants were cowering back under overhangs and shielding their eyes against the nearby bare lightbulbs and peering up into the darkness, trying to see who it was, this voice that was laughing down on them, the one who had done this, like stoning them.

"Nancy!" cried Cash. "What are you *do*ing?"

Nancy was laughing, and she kept on laughing, a ringing, resounding, haunting laugh. Well, the explosion of the fish tank had stunned them, and now Nancy's vindictive act was electrifying them. They were conglomerating for safety under the balcony across from mine and they were all talking at once—all but Cash. She was out in the middle of the floor on her knees, rocking back and forth, crying and yelling to everyone in general, "Don't *touch* anything, don't *touch* anything." Then she got to her feet and went staggering about through the mess, sloshing through this puddle of silt, weed, fish and ooze, like trying to comprehend it.

Then—with a crack and a splat—something hit the floor near her feet and went bouncing away. She went after it and came out from under my balcony holding a metal figurine, holding it toward the laughing Nancy and shaking it at her. And suddenly Cash was going up the main stairs, carrying this figurine like a club, like she was going to catch Nancy and clobber her over the head with it.

178

And as if this were some kind of signal, all hell broke loose—the elegants dispersed in all directions and went every way but out. Some raced up the main stairway after Cash, others ran toward the front of the house; a few went around the main room knocking things over and kicking things around, and as I was sitting there Indian fashion on my balcony wrapped in the beach towel, I heard pounding feet on the stairway behind me, and here came a pack of them. Diogenes went scratching off into his dark corner and was crouched there hissing when the first of them reached the top of our stairs, turned the bend and thumped on down the hallway. A line of them went by that way, their faces slack, like they were being blown along by some inner desperation—what I'd seen in them before, what had been the undercurrent in their gangbang celebration. Well, it was now clearly to the surface and like a military commander it had them all moving to its order, was turning them into a horde of starving peasants storming the castle's pantry.

That, roughly, is what it looked like from here; we were witnessing, Diogenes and I, the revolt of the Ids, the overthrow of the *Shoulds*. A Sin-erama in spectacular three-D. Like they were out in some Far West of their natures and their fronts, their put-ons, had given way to something neither good nor evil, but the opposite side of that coin— the Is, Was, Always Will Be of themselves.

A hot, pungent mixture of odors from their bodies washed over me as they went past, their movements quick, clean, agile, heated by the excitement of their new possibilities. For this was no ordinary revolution; the spirit of it seemed to have a force like tons of water that had just

179

broken from a dam and was roaring along in an unstoppable torrent that would sweep everything in its path.

As one girl reached my balcony—the one who'd taken off her blouse—the kitchen phone rang, which slowed her long enough to bare her teeth at me and cackle an otherworldly laugh before she went dashing down the hall after the others. It was a strange laugh, a threatening laugh, and I hadn't heard its like since one night a couple of years ago when I saw a woman get put into a mad sexual heat by watching two men slugging it out over her, and it occurred to me that the lot of them were possessed by something at once sexual and violent, like they really did believe violence and sex are one, the one the essence of the other. Or else like they were using violence to overthrow their sexual restraints and sex to power the drive of their violence—who knows? Anyhow, whatever was going on in them, it was clear from the looks on their faces, the quickness of their movements, that they were going on this binge in a state of do-or-die desperation inspired by some keen need that gave not one good goddamn for tomorrow. Truly, it was an uplifting sight; I realized they'd all be full of their usual good cheer again come next Christmas, but for the moment they were a world away from the fancy clothes of their hypocrisy, that peace-on-earth, goodwill-to-men they shout as they drop their bombs and liberate people from life.

When the last of them had rounded the bend and was gone down the hall, Diogenes slipped out of his shadow and came trotting over and hopped affectionately up on my lap. I was flattered, of course; we sat there listening to the noises coming from the bowels of the house—there was

180

bashing and battering like two dozen carpenters furiously at work. Bangs and clatters, splinterings of wood and crashings of glass—surely enough audio-visual goings-on to put a movie director chewing his megaphone. I almost expected to hear the whine and buzzing of an electric saw next, as they pressed on into the sheety sanctum of this house and battered these leavings of European antiquity.

Suddenly, out of the hall came a big beefy elegant, straining under the weight of a marble podium held up over his head like a barbell, his face flushed and contorted with effort; Diogenes shoved off against my stomach and ran for cover again as this guy staggered forward with his load. He made it to the railing and tottered, looking down, then he gave a little bounce of his legs and heaved it off and down it went to land with a floor-smashing, glass-crashing, water-splattering crack and kerrumph.

As the reverberations of this died away in echoes, the phone gave a bleating, demanding ring, and from right below my balcony came a blood-curdling scream. Some girl down there sounded like she thought that podium was meant to crush her.

Well, the husky departed then and out came another—this one panting and groaning, carrying an armful of little figurines and a wooden slat—I guess he'd ripped it from a window shutter. He put down his load of figurines in a neat pile, he acknowledged my blanketed presence with a demented chuckle and he set to work. Wielding the slat like a baseball bat, he tossed a figurine into the air and whacked it out off the balcony, like hitting a fly ball to some faraway leftfield of his imagination. Most of the figurines shattered to bits at the crack of his bat, but some managed to get off—one staying intact completely, a high fly to the edge of the third-floor balcony where Nancy-baby reached out and down trying to field it but it bumped the edge of her balcony and fell to the carpeting of the main stairway, bounced down the steps to the floor and sat there, good as new.

Next upon my balcony came a girl, a redhead with her hair piled on top of her head and a blue ribbon in it; she was wearing glasses that kept sliding down her short nose and almost falling off the end of it, and her wet clothes were clinging to her body. She carried an empty display case, picked from a wall somewhere, and with a squeaky little noise of glee that sounded like "Mee-oie," she swung and tossed it over the railing, like off the stern of a ship, then she turned and went briskly back down the hall.

By now I was dumfounded, numb with fascination at this new turn their celebration was taking, and the violent, rapacious possibilities it suggested were getting to me. So I followed my curiosity down the hall for a look-see.

Poking my head into the first room I came to I found a pair of them, boy and girl, methodically smashing everything they could lay their hands on. The boy had a wooden slat in his hands and was swinging it, knocking things flying off tables, then chopping down at them and axing away at whatever grabbed his attention while the girl was going along the other wall, pulling drawers out of bureaus and spilling their contents, picking things up, flinging them down, or, if they were large enough to get a good grip on, bashing them against the wall.

The room leading to the outside balcony had already been thoroughly wrecked and forgotten. I went through it,

182

crunching over broken glass with the soles of my shoes and kicking larger pieces of the wreckage out of my path, to the balcony where two boys and a girl were diligently trying to hoist a bedframe into position to heave it over the railing and down onto the patio. At the far end of this balcony lay a mattress with a couple side by side on it. I saluted them with my martini, took a sip and moved on, back through the room and on down the hall, checking all the rooms to my left as I went. Most of them had already been ravished, their doors left ajar, their crew of wreckers departed. At the end of the hall, light still came from the cracks around the door to the caretakers' apartment, and from inside it still came the incredible sound of TV. I leaned against their door for a moment to marvel at this, then I toasted the doorknob with my glass, sipped and started back.

The story was the same in the first couple of rooms on the other side of the hall—doors ajar, wrecking going on or done with. Then I came to a door which was closed; I put an ear to it, but with all the noise around me I could hear nothing from the other side of it, so I opened it slowly and peered in. Here, sheets had been piled neatly in the middle of the floor and around the room there was the usual wreckage. Then, going on into the room I saw a bed out of some past century with a couple of copulators on it. They were violating each other furiously, going at it with gusto; his pants were down around his ankles and she had an arm draped ladylike over his back, and in her fingertips she held her panties, which, moved by their steady thrusting, waved and fluttered at me gaily.

I closed their door quietly and moved on, and when I

poked my head into the next room, there was what looked
like two bareassed babes playing horsey. I mean here on
the floor mid the wreckage of this room were these two
chicks, one behind the other, both facing the same direction, and what they were riding was a guy. One girl had
herself astride his hips and the other his face, so his cock
was in the cunt of one and his tongue in the cunt of the
other, and he was making sounds like he was having trouble
breathing—because the girl over his face was being a bit
overbearing. Both of these elegant daughters were relishing
their relations with this potential bolt in the power structure, and the one who was doing her little belly dance on
his hips lifted her face to me and smiled pleasantly, like
inviting me into the game. I remembered her from the
patio—she was the one who'd wryly said sex, sex and more
sex, it's really very boring. But that was a book she'd been
talking about and now that she was getting herself a boring
in her own sex, she seemed just plain delighted, and the
smile she turned on me tempted me to become one of them
and make it a foursome.

But it was a moral and aesthetic temptation I was feeling, and what was pleasing me was imagining myself astride
them all, being sucked off by the hip-rider, and half-sitting
on the back and shoulders of the muff-rider, thereby holding
them all down, like reversing the way it is in real life. For
it did fascinate the be-jesus out of me to come upon this
inheritor of social domination dominated by these two
squirming dollies, but I had no real physical desire for it
just then, so I only thought about it—was standing there
watching it with the smile of the hip-rider on me and the
muffled sounds of the guy coming at me when, from the

dark at the far end of the room I heard fitful, frightened cries: "Ooh! Ahhh! Oooh! Oh, oh-my-god, *no*. I *cain't*. It won't *fit*."

A girl, and she sounded slightly hysterical, and another girl was answering her in a calm, reassuring voice: "Yes it will, Jill. Just relax. Go ahead, MacDonald, push. Come on, push."

I made my way through a pile of smashed relics to the far corner and here was another threesome. One girl was on her knees with her butt up and her head down in the triangular crack of the corner; a guy was behind her on his knees and another girl was crawling around the pair of them like a busy mechanic. She was trying to make it work, trying to get the guy to squeeze it into the asshole of the first girl.

I stood over the scene watching it, unnoticed. The guy, I saw, was the one who'd been talking about making a responsible decision and taking a position and making a commitment. Well, they'd made a responsible decision, okay, and a position had been taken, and the scene looked ripe for a commitment. It clicked in my brain that there was some kind of basic morality being enacted here. I wasn't sure what. But the guy was having a hell of a time committing himself up her ass.

But if the girl-mechanic had her way she was going to *make* it work—he was by God going to get himself committed. She was having no shillyshallying—when her girlfriend tried to get out of her position, the girl-mechanic responded by assuming the responsibility of shoving her head back down into the corner. And when the guy showed signs of giving up the whole idea and quitting, she ran

185

around behind him—like if he wasn't going to push forward into his commitment she was going to push him in herself.

While she was pushing I tapped her on the shoulder and she juked like the place was being raided by her hometown vice squad. I said, "Got any Vaseline?"

She sprang from her knees and stood there confronting me in a panicky stance, and she wailed, "What?"

"Vaseline."

She stared dumfounded and I saw that she was the one who'd said that women are people too.

Then, wham! I heard a sharp slap and felt the sting on my face and I realized she'd just slapped me. Not hard but it was enough of a distraction to send me away and to undo the not-quite-done coupling on the floor—the two of them were on their feet and all three were talking at once as I took my solemn leave.

Enough random sampling, I said to myself. Women are people and people are people and Vaseline is Vaseline, and one of these days that daughter of advanced social advantage might advance in other ways too, but for the time being I'd have to leave her with her abrasive communications problem unlubricated, for she wasn't about to take any tips from me.

Maybe it's just my own peculiar past experience, but it seemed to me, now, as I wandered back toward my balcony, that the closer I got to the confiscators of our material wealth, the rougher, more sado-masochistic the sex scenes became. Back at those parties we used to have with those colored girls everything happened so velvety smooth and soft and gentle, like in a high where you felt you were gliding on clouds. No quick, jerky motions—no one made a fast move till the other was with it and both were on the come and making it together on the same beat. And then on to the university and Arnold and his chicks, especially the one from the highclass girls college who loved to be pinched and bitten like straight out of tales of the Marquis de Sade, and now to that business on the floor of that room, the one who'd just slapped me at the mention of Vaseline.

Must be their upbringing, I thought. All part of the psychological equipment they need to play the role they should—to deal with the rest of society like it's theirs to raid and plunder and be benevolent toward.

I remembered this one richbitch I played with at the swim club—she used to provoke me, do anything to get me to hurt her. That was her kink and I still had two scars on my arm where she'd put the lighted ends of cigarettes into me, trying to put me in a rage. Which she finally did and then we had this big bopping scene and she screamed and cried and afterward came cuddling up to me practically purring. It put me wondering what it would be like to be married to her. Sure would make a guy tough physically, but *lord!* what a mess he'd become otherwise —the sort of mess a man must be to relish his role as a plunderer, maybe. Her duty to her class.

Well, the truth of the matter is, I got more of a thrill out of belting that bitch around than I like to admit. It was enough of a thrill to show me I could make that scene and play that uppercrusty role. Enough to make me realize, too, how *un*moral old Mother Creation really is, and how blood-lusty are her human offspring, how

187

delicate, thin, transparent is the veil between rapacious murder and the marvels of the joyous passions, how practically one-and-the-same they are. The human predicament.

Anyhow, I was back on my balcony with Diogenes; he'd returned and was sitting on his haunches with his old serenity, gazing down at the main room, the end of his tail flopping back and forth contentedly. Which caused me to suppose his good instincts had it that these fine young aristocrats would not disturb him further, now that their roving wrecking had brought them to fucking, sucking and sodomizing.

He greeted me with a glance and watched me put my damp clothes back on. Then his cat's candor got to me—he was being just too damned smug about it. I hoisted my glass to him and said, "Diogenes, come off that self-righteousness. Violence is a kick for cats too, you know. I've seen you mothahs battle over puss."

He turned away with that, as if to tell me that the mating-time battles of him and his kind are a far cry from what these elegant sons and daughters of the rich and powerful were up to here.

"You may have a point," I said. "At least, I hope so. I hope it's that they're denatured and not getting renatured."

And Diogenes looked up at me as if to say, who the hell are you trying to kid?

So I split—couldn't take his argumentative silence. Parked my elegant longstemmed glass of martini carefully on a flat spot on the railing top and went off for further explorations.

From the other wing of the house now I could hear,

mid the subsiding bang-clatter-crashing of their methodical wrecking, the far-off sound of Cash, hollering at her wild-gone guests. She sounded weird, like a Protestant who's been dropped into Purgatory and is trying to contact the cosmos to complain about such a mad mistake.

Just before I started down the hallway to the other wing, I heard a voice behind me and turned, and there was the Lover, the guy; he was saying, "Where's Nancy-baby? You seen Nancy-baby?" and he was grinning broadly, like a stuffedshirt of a husband who's letting down his hair and is out on the town, cheating on his wife.

"I haven't seen her," I said—as I checked to make sure she was still leaning over the railing of the third-floor balcony opposite mine. But he was in a trance and acted like he didn't care what I might have to say; he just wandered on, sort of chanting, "Where's Nancy-baby, where's Nancy-baby."

Then I was off through the dark hallway, groping along its walls, headed for the other wing. And about halfway through it another figure came at me from the far end. He was rushing along, stumbling over fallen objects and banging into displaced tables, like he was fleeing. I pressed myself against the wall to give him plenty of passing room; he was making grunting noises and panting like he'd just been in a fight. Or was looking for a fight—anyway, I didn't want to tangle with him nohow. He saw me, though, and stopped, and we were on either side of a table that, strangely enough, had gone untouched. So now this big beefy grunting aristocrat grabbed the sheet that covered it and gave a grunting yank, sending stuff crashing to the floor. Then he stood there laughing—like "Aurrr, harrr,

harrr!"—right in my face, sharing the joke. But when I didn't laugh back he shut up and went on his way, making some new sound.

"Brotherhood week in the American nuthouse," I said to his departing back, and I peeled myself from the wall and went on.

At the end of the hall I bumped smack into Arnold, and with him was—to my keen amazement—Mary. She was still wearing that big plumed hat with the white feather hanging jauntily down by her ear, and Arnold had her by the hand and was taking her somewhere. He greeted me with a big grin and a "Hey! Look who I found!"

"Congratulations."

"You want seconds?"

"No thanks."

"Well, if you change your mind, she'll be in the last room on the right."

Like she was a carcass and we were vultures.

Then he brushed past me pulling her along behind; she was turning her head this way and that like a child being hustled through a busy department store, and she was peering into each room as she went by it, hurried on by Arnold.

In the other direction down the hall I saw the vague silhouette of a guy, just standing there doing nothing; I went toward him. He was the one who'd said I wasn't one of them and neither was he, and now here he was, still not one of them and neither was I. Though he was out of it for reasons much different than mine.

And the next moment he was not out of it, for Cash

popped from a room, spotted the guy and was rushing him like a wildcat, making noises deep in her throat as she came. And then I heard a ripping sound and there was Cash, holding a piece of the guy's shirt and the guy was pleading with her: "What are you doing? Cash, what are you doing?" She was going after another piece of his shirt—at which point the guy decided to defend himself; he caught her by the wrists and they waltzed around in the hallway for a while, Cash making that noise deep in her throat and the guy saying, "Now stop that, Cash. Cool down, will you? What's the matter with you?"

Then Cash sort of gave up and slumped, and if the guy hadn't caught hold of her under the arms she'd have fallen to the floor. Well, he just stood there supporting her for a second or two like he was immobilized, and then he saw me. And like he felt duty-bound to protect her reputation from the likes of me, he dragged her on down the hall and into the nearest room, out of my sight and hearing. I went to the door and closed it behind them, wishing them both the best.

And when I turned from doing that I was face to face with someone else, a female. A panting, hot-breathed female. I drew back and saw that it was Vallery, her blond hair in disarray, and she was huffing and puffing, baring her teeth and looking at me through half-closed eyes. She was coming on like she had rape in mind and her hands were already under my shirt and clutching my bare back. Mine went quick and automatic into her torn blouse and in the spirit the party had become I was giving her neat, firm little breasts a hefty mugging when I felt her fingers

191

at the zipper of my pants. I took time out to help these gropers reach their playmate and then sent my right hand up her dress and was being so carried away that I was about to plug in and become one of them—was even tugging her pants down and getting positioned to shove it to her right here and now, when—screaming hysterically toward us out of the room nearby came Cash, and before I could get untangled from Vallery's skirts and on the run, Cash's claws were in me—she had a handful of hair and was yanking my head back and forth, and was digging the fingernails of her other hand into the skin of my neck.

Vallery split and scurried away down the hall in a fit of giggles, and the guy who'd dragged Cash into the room came out and was helping me get loose. He had her by the wrists again and was talking soothingly to her: "Now Cash, don't do this thing—it's terrible the way you're behaving, now stop it."

I couldn't hang on long enough to let him get the job done his way; I let fly a punch backward at her ribs and that did the trick quick. She was on the floor, moaning, and the guy was bending over her solicitously, so I left them to deal with their own strangulated libidos.

My instinct now was to find Vallery and fuck her; I took off down the hall after her and was peering into this room and that, trying to spot that particular torn blouse in the wreckage and among the swirl of elegant torn clothes and seminude or nude bodies that I was seeing dimly in the dark of these rooms, when she came at me again— Cash, shrieking out of the darkness with her hands raised and her fingernails poised like after a quick kill. This time I caught her by the wrists and held her till the guy got to

192

us and pinned her arms behind her back. She kept struggling and kicking out—forward at my shins and backward at his—and yelling, "See what you *did! See?*"

"... *I* did!"

"Are you *happy* now? *Are* you?"

"What are you talking about—*I* did."

"Augh, awwk, ooooh," and more noises from the back of her throat. "You *bas*tard! You *sun*uvabitch! *You* did it, *you* did it!"

By this time the other guy and I had sort of an understanding, so I said, "Hold her till I get out of here." Then I moved away, walking backward. She was still struggling furiously and letting fly an occasional kick when I reached the hall to the other wing and ducked into it.

I groped my way back, wondering if by *you* she really did mean me. Me personally. Me alone. It seemed very definitely like that is exactly what she meant, like she'd somehow gotten it in her elegant richbitch head that *I* had brought all this on.

16

IT HAD ME FEELING all tied up tight in body and mind. I didn't know what to make of it—how in the world she ever got that idea—and I was tempted to turn back and have it out with her. If she was trying to turn me onto a rage and get me to knock her around and all that, okay; it wouldn't be the first time I'd played that game with one of those daughters, and the thought of beating Cash around did, I'll admit, tempt me. If that's what she wants . . .

But no. I told myself to cool it, loosen up, breathe deep and easy—that their sado-masochistic ways weren't for me. Would only make me one of them. And I was groping my way back through the connecting hallway and trying to wind down and come off that tight feeling; I was whistling a snide, off-key rendition of "Dixie" and telling myself that all I really wanted out of this housewrecking-cum-orgy was a good fast fuck. Or maybe two, but to get all boxed in knocking Cash around was a personal danger I didn't need, and a waste of time into the bargain. If the bitch comes on me again, I thought, I'll offer to fuck her up the ass and thereby de-bitch her some—sort of put the finishing touches on this assault on the asshole of their glorious

194

culture, this housewrecking by her friends and fellow aristocrats. Yeah, I'll offer her that, but I won't let her put me in her trickbag.

I was deep in such funky thoughts as these when I reached my balcony and retrieved my martini, saluted Diogenes and drained the glass—and saw, through the elegant longstemmed crystal bottom of the empty glass as I held it to my lips, none other than Judy girl clown. Coming at me out of the hall with quick, sprightly steps and a pert smile. The only aftereffects of her drenched knighthood were her caked and matted hair and soaked clothes; otherwise, she was glowing happily, looking like the fresh-skinned girl in the shower on the TV ad.

"Hi," she chirped. Like greeting a friend between classes, real bright and bushy-tailed, gazing grinningly into my eyes.

So, I said to myself, here's my quickie. I put down my glass and was about to take her to one of the rooms—but didn't. It was like looking at something, blinking, then looking at it again and seeing it as something else. For on my second look, her gleefulness came like cold water to my passions. With Cash's curses ringing in my ear, what would I do with *this?* This happy one—somehow she wasn't one of them either. And the unhappy truth of it was, *I* was becoming one of them. Was into it enough now to be itching for a bitch I could hatefuck, not looking for a girl who was happy and full of joy and ready to go after her goodies with a sense of fun.

And all of this must have been plain as day on my face, for Judy took off—suddenly just left me standing there

195

and marched back the way she'd come—back down the hall in search of some other and, hopefully, less grim partner for the orgy.

So here I was alone, leaning against the balcony's railing, listening to the sounds of the housewrecking subsiding as more of them moved from one form of their sex-violence to the other. One couple, I saw when I turned around, was against the railing of the third-floor balcony across the main room—right where Nancy had been—and they were going at it in one position, then another, like out of a stag flick. Below them, on the second-floor balcony, was Cash; she was leaning on the railing, resting her face in the palms of her hands, staring down at the mess below like someone leaning out of a tenement window watching the goings-on in the street.

Then, down in front of my eyes floated a shirt—somebody's tattered shirt fluttering down to land in the slime and ooze of the puddle of wreckage on the main floor. And from behind me now came the loud laughter of a girl. Judy, maybe. And soon all around me were sounds and sights that suggested that all these mainstream members of the party had, at last, smashed their way through to what they wanted—the horde of starving peasants had reached the castle's pantry and were gorging themselves.

Well, I said to myself, if you're going to get yours, you'd best get a-goin'. Down that hall and find yourself a partner and make the scene, man, 'cause if you don't get on your way right soon, it'll be too late.

And that's when I knew that for me it was gone, for I no longer had *any* desire.

196

Come on, I told myself, you can't watch it and do it *both*, you have to watch it *or* do it, one or the other.

But myself was too deep in a blue funk. I just stayed there watching the performing pair across the way, hearing the noise level subside from bangs and clatters to occasional laughter. I wasn't even itching for a bitch now. I was numb, out of it, somewhere else. Like the wind had gone out of the sails for me and I was in a state of motionless blah.

It was like the time in my childhood when the wind had gone out of the sails for our family; the farm was gone and all we had left was the house. Then Pappy lost his job and we were rock-bottom broke with nowhere to go, no getaway money, no grocery money, no hope. Only welfare. We were seven stranded souls on a big ocean in a small sailboat and there wasn't any wind, not the slightest breeze. And suddenly lost from our lives were those Sunday afternoons when Pappy would slyly interrupt Mama's bath in the kitchen, and she'd hop out, grab a towel and make a run for it. He'd chase her and the rest of us would chase the two of them, catching a fit of giggles from them, and then they'd escape us into the bedroom and we'd press our ears against the door and listen to their laughter subside and turn into the rhythmic singing and creaking of the bedsprings and the thump of the bedstead hitting the wall. Such Sundays had an uplifting effect on our whole family—always put the suspicion in the air that they'd result in something, like maybe a new brother or sister, and even when they didn't there was something about them that had implications of on-goingness. But suddenly

197

they were gone—when Pappy's labor was no longer found profitable to the papers of incorporation that owned the mill, our family on-goingness got lost and we didn't have those Sunday afternoons any more—the line of us in size order romping through the house chasing Mama's bare behind—and it wasn't long afterward that their car went over the bridge.

Well, here and now there was that same something smelling of a bad ending. My life at the university and the highrising bit I'd gotten into—it was like I'd been on a long crosscountry trip that led to this, this impasse, and it was now time to declare that unless I took a different route I'd never make it over the Donner Pass. Others could go this route no doubt, but not me, not me. I need something else.

It was while mulling over this that I felt eyes at my back and turned, and found Nancy-baby standing near the top of my stairs, watching me. I don't know what brought her, nor how long she'd been standing here, but now she came toward me with a look that said it all—that here we were, the two horniest ones at this party, and now look.

She leaned against the railing beside me and we stayed side by side in a comfortable silence, directly across from where Cash was.

After a while, Nancy said, "I don't understand what's happening. It makes me sick. Makes me not want to live. It's all so . . . so un*nor*mal, so *ab*normal. I mean, why are they *do*ing all this? Did someone put LSD in the martini or something? I mean, how did it *happ*en?"

"Someone *should* have put LSD in the martini," I tried. But she wasn't on my side of that.

"No! I'm serious!" she said.

Which put uppermost in my mind the question I didn't ask her. Not out loud, but she was looking into my eyes and must have read me, for she said, "Me, what happened to me I can understand. I may not know how to put it into words but I *know*. Yes, I know about *that*." Then her eyes searched mine so intently I felt like she was trying to see into my soul. "You weren't one of them, were you. On the beach, I mean."

"No. I was the one fetched you the clothes. Remember?"

"I know, I know. But, I mean . . . why? Why weren't you with them on the beach?"

"Because, I'm not one of *them*."

I guess she heard that her way, not mine. But whatever it came out meaning to her, she said, "That's sweet." And she put her hand on my head and began twining my hair around in her fingers.

"I'm sorry about what happened to you," I said.

"But it *had* to happen."

"What do you mean?"

"I don't know . . . it just *had* to. Cash tried so *hard* to stop it, she tried so *hard*." Then she got lost in thought for a moment. "It's funny, isn't it. The way people are."

"*Which* people?"

"Me, you, everybody. I wonder what's going to become of us."

"People? We'll pass into compost like a trillion more before us."

"I mean, what's going to happen to *my* life? Like, how did I get *into* this? Cash says I'm a . . . I'm sick . . . nympho . . . maniac."

"I don't buy that. You're not the sick one, they are. All of them."

She smiled on me like a big sister tolerating a childish opinion from a favorite little brother. And that provoked me. "Nancy, how can you *accept* what happened to you? Those vicious sons of bitches, they—"

"Oh, *no!* No, you can't call them that. And I can't pretend it was all *their* fault. I mean you weren't *here* for the other two parties—that's when it all began. Cash says I brought it on myself, but . . . that's not it either. I mean, you know, even back when I was twelve everyone as*sumed* I was a sexpot. They'd take one look at me and assume I was a *sex*pot. And like you're always surrounded by people who think you are a certain something and pretty soon you become what they think you are. It's like you don't have any *choice*. They won't *let* you be anything *else*. And all you can do is say, oh what the hell. And when you *do* become what they think you are they turn *against* you. It's crazy."

I felt some truth in that, but I said, "That's bullshit! You can go away, go somewhere and get among different people and become a different person."

"No, no you can't—not me. I tried. Spent all last summer in Mexico trying to be somebody else and it didn't work. It was even *worse*. I mean I just gave up down there. Came back *me,* nobody else *but* me, the same old sexpot." She picked the empty glass out of my hand and tipped it for its last drop. "No, you're wrong and so is Cash, and so is everybody."

"But you're letting them tell you what to be, Nancy. Don't you *see* that?"

200

"Sure I see that, but what choice do I have?" She shook her head and brushed the hanging hair back from her face. "Oh I'm so *tired* of it all. I wish it were different, but it isn't. It really isn't."

Then she left me and went walking away like someone stoned on pot and disappeared into the darkness of the hall, and the last I heard of her, she said, "I wish I had a choice but I don't. Nobody does."

Nobody does: that shook me. For I could find in my own life just enough truth in that to make it stick. Like back in the institution where I was what they called an incorrigible—they classed me as an incorrigible and I was. When I first heard the word I thought it meant, like, encourageable—undiscourageable or unpigeonholeable— and I accepted it as a badge to be worn with considerable pride, for it was my instinct to stay as un-had by them as possible, to keep a free spirit lit inside me even while they had me marching to their orders and putting on like a tomming grin and shuffle for them.

And I had gotten myself into my share of trouble— going AWOL the first week they put me in that place, going around sullen and homesick for the fields I'd romped in, and for the muddy river and the foggy mornings and how the wild flowers in the springtime practically talk to you when you're alone with them in the field. And somehow in my first miseries I got into the habit of stealing money from the housemasters and governesses—they all slept with their doors open and I'd wake up in the wee hours and sneak down the hall and make the rounds, and I'd accumulated over a hundred dollars before I got caught one night—in the room of the prettiest governess with my grubby little paw in her pocketbook. Which turned out to be a thrilling experience, for she woke up and came bouncing warmly out of bed and grabbed me and I got to bury myself in her sheerly nightgowned bosom and beg for sympathy, and we must have had a mutual thing going for she hugged me to her and held me, then she took me over to her bed and embraced and lectured me as I wriggled and squirmed against her, and that went on till dawn. But they'd caught their mystery thief that night, and they never forgot it, and from there on out I was marked. Whenever somebody'd done something and they were hunting for the culprit, they'd line us up and say, "Okay, who did it?" And if nobody owned up, they'd yank me out of line and cuff me around. They even pinned the blame on me for things they *knew* I hadn't done, as if I'd somehow spooked it into happening. It got to be pretty ridiculous, since I was committing all sorts of horrendous rule-breakings and getting away with most of them, while at the same time they were blaming me for things I hadn't done. So I spent a good bit of my teenage energy playing a game of broken-field running against the rulers, figuring out what they expected me to do and doing pretty much the opposite, trying to keep the scales of poetic justice tipped in my favor. And so they had told me too who to be, and what choice did I have?

Well, having been such a number-one scapegoat and played that game with them for so many years—what they call the formative years—being blamed by Cash for what was going on at this party did, I had to admit, satisfy. It was like attending a political party convention that had been carefully rigged and is coming off exactly as you'd

202

have made it come off if you'd been the one to rig it—but since you hadn't even known it was rigged, all you can be is happily amazed. At which point, someone tells you it's your fault.

And what made this thing even more delightful for me was what had gotten wrecked. The sort of things I'd always associated with the powers—those irrelevant art objects I always felt an urge to smash or deface. For not only were they the property of, but in some subtle way I felt they were the *tools* of those powers—those emperors, kings, millionaires, politicians—all those the likes of me are forced to serve. Those bastards we've died in wars for, those motherfuckers who can order the world blown to smithereens any moment now.

So here I sat, the poorboy at the party, where the sons and daughters of the rich and powerful had smashed the artifacts of the rich and powerful and had misused the richest of their beauties. Had turned the tables on themselves. How could I be anything but delightfully satisfied?

And yet, now that the noisy business of the housewrecking was all gone and the relative calm of the orgy was upon us, and as I sat on my haunches beside the wise Diogenes and surveyed the wreckage that made the main floor a weird, rubble-ridden meeting place where stone faces out of the Roman Empire sat in conference with plumed helmets out of the Middle Ages, where the sleek stone form of an Athenian chick lay naked near the cold metal that had encased the passions of some knight, where the statue of that mighty horse decked out for the tilting contest stood conspicuously by as if waiting for a rider, for one of those fallen stone or metal forms to rise up out of that rubble,

203

climb into its big saddle and go galloping off—and, as rising up out of this mess came the stink of the silt that had been at the bottom of the aquarium, the seaweed, dead and dying fish, and mingled with this the finer, cleaner odors of splintered wood and the powders of smashed stone, I became aware of some sorrow in myself. A feeling of letdown that I couldn't account for. Surely I had to be happy with what had happened—what else could I be? And if she wanted to put the blame for it all on me—well, shouldn't that be just an extra added delight?

But if it was, I wasn't feeling it. Now I was feeling a letdown, like I'd been cheated, or like my prejudice just wasn't sturdy enough to hold up under this.

I told myself there was no point in sitting here feeling a damned thing over this wreckage, this pile of what had been the pretentious sheet-covered objects her father had the shitcovered legalistics to claim he owned. As if it's possible to buy with their money the sort of wealth an artist invests in an object. Especially when most of the objects he had here were copies, only copies. Out of the bygones of the European culture they'd transplanted to America where those old assumptions less than didn't suit us, had killed thousands of us and driven practically all of us mad.

And yet . . . I thought of the circle of her father's phony Greeks out on the patio. They'd been phonied up and bowdlerized to a fare-thee-well, true; still, I liked them, valued them, found something ironic in them standing there from out of their Greco-Roman Americanized mythical antiquity. For I wanted to imagine them being from a more practical time, a more humane time of being in tune with life as it is; I wanted to see them as standing there

204

watching these materially overprivileged young moderns with their great and murderous campaigns against the natural and cosmic order, and their style of killing their own best impulses. And I wanted the spirit of my Greeks— my own vision of her father's phony Greeks—with me in the roaring loathing I felt in my blood and bones for these sons and daughters of the rich and powerful, in my searing, spooky prayer that their ways will bring them to such an orgy of self-destruction that the rest of us will be rid of them once and for all. For I wanted to imagine a real Grecian time when our illustrious species was hip to the fact that the best we can hope for is to take care of ourselves and all that is creation's, including our own most pleasing creations.

But that's not what the inheritors of wealth and power will ever allow to happen, and I knew it. And so I felt the letdown—because even as I watched my dream for them simulated here at this party, I knew it was not their final blast, that tomorrow they'd be going on about their business: serving the collective deathwish, playing their game of cops and robbers like a dog chasing its own tail. Making the rest of us catch their particular strain of the human disease, leading our great stampede to self-destruction.

17

AND SO THE FEELING of letdown. But my thoughts put me on my feet and sent me on my way downstairs to find out what had become of that circle of phony Greeks. I went sloshing and fumbling through the rubble toward the doors to the patio—three of the six of them had been smashed—and I stepped outside through the frame of a smashed one, and there they were, miraculously intact. Completely untouched. Even unscratched.

Glass from the doors lay in small pieces all around and a mattress sat upright in the fountain's water, propped against the back of a male statue. But the cherub still had that silly stream of water gushing from his mouth and the eight naked stone youths still stood like they'd been caught and petrified while arriving for a friendly orgy.

I went over and hauled the mattress out, dragged it over the patio and heaved it over the planter wall onto the beach.

Then, from inside, I heard a series of softer and evenly spaced sounds—thump . . . thump . . . thump, plus an occasional bang-clatter. I went back into the main room and there was Cash at the top of the stairs, tossing down the overnight bags and clothes of the boys, and now and then a waterski or surfboard. Tossing them into the middle of the puddle on the main floor. When she saw me, she pointed to the sliding glass doors and said, "Well, go ahead, break another one—go ahead."

I stepped back out to the patio and wandered around for a while, then I went into the kitchen area; it had come through the war relatively unsmashed. I was behind the partition thinking of fixing myself something to eat when I heard a new series of sounds; I poked my head around and now Cash was popping in and out of the door to the girls' room, tossing out overnight bags and pocketbooks, towels, panties, bras, adding them to the mess in the middle of the floor.

Well, it was her problem, all hers; I'm not one of them and I ain't about to become one of them, so I might as well reward myself with a little bite to eat. There was a larger-than-real-life refrigerator here in the kitchen and it yielded me slices of fresh lunchmeat, then I located mustard and some bread. I came upon an electric coffee-maker in a big walk-in closet, and a can of coffee, so I set a full pot to brewing, chuckling at an imagined scene: me serving coffee to the elegants as they stood about in the main-room rubble, their chins up, backs straight, stiff-upper-lipped and clothes all tattered and torn. Wouldn't that be a gas? I could hear them now, going through their bright, witty chit-chattings and neon smilings following their festival of fucking.

I fixed myself one sandwich and ate it while the coffee was a-making, then I made another and took it and my cup of coffee out to the patio and sat down on the steps to the beach. It was the crack of dawn; I was hearing the wake-up chirps of birds and through the gray morning light

207

I could just make out the white-capped tips of rollers as they crested to break and came foaming in. Like they'd always done and would go on doing—it made me glad to think what little power the rich and powerful have over the cosmic heaving and churning of the sea.

Then I heard a small scratching sound from one corner of the patio, and in the shadows over there I discovered Diogenes: that utterly practical fellow, he was breakfasting on fish.

After the sandwich and coffee I felt sleepy, so I leaned back against the end of the planter wall and nodded off, lulled by the steady pounding of the surf. It was a light sleep; I never lost the sound of the surf, but it had a dream in it for me. I was back with the first love of my life, Rosie, when we were teenagers meeting in the park down by the river and going through that first time of passions so intense and incredible I didn't think I'd live through them. Rosie's the color of the fields I used to "help" my Pappy plow back when I was barely big enough to ride the tractor axle, and the truth of it is I cultivated her. But she's gone forever, I guess. She always went by whatever last name was most convenient, and by now she might be an X. I met her when I was sixteen at one of those integrated parties we used to have; we sort of bumped into each other in the dark and we danced, and as soon as I put my arms around her and felt her tight against me, I knew how young, dumb and full of come I really was, because I hadn't known there were feelings like this in life to be had. Worlds opened to me, and I suspect it was pretty much the same for her, though we never discussed it; we came together and we clung together for over a year.

We had a certain place in the city park that was ours—
it was a big bush beside the bridle path overlooking the
river, and we could crawl under the branches of the bush
and feel like we were in our own little house. We'd make
a bed of newspaper and have a honeymoon. At night and
even on certain Saturday afternoons while people rode
back and forth on horses a few feet from us. We thought
we had the whole world fooled until one weekday night—
a parkguard followed her as she left the ghetto and came
into the park to meet me; he must have sneaked along right
behind her because about a minute after she'd ducked into
our little bush house and we were hugging each other for
dear life, the son of a bitch shined his light on us and
ordered us out. He took us to a cop car and they drove
us to the station house, and they all stood around grinning
and asking questions like, "What were you *doing* in the
bushes?" They didn't want to book us, they just wanted to
haze us, and they did until they had us both as terrified
as lost children, and then they let us go out into the strange
streets of a white neighborhood on the other side of the
park, and we weren't sure how to get home from there. I
walked on one side of the street and she on the other, and
we went for miles like that, all the way around the park to
her ghetto, then we sat down side by side on a curb and
cried. Just sat there with tears running down our cheeks
till the morning light came, then we split. She went home
and I sneaked back to the orphanage.

We only saw each other a couple of times after that,
for her mother decided to move to Detroit and Rosie
went with her. But a few months later, her girlfriend told
me she knew somebody from Detroit who said Rosie was

going to have a baby. That put me in a daze, and when I came out of it I was frantic to hitchhike to Detroit and find her, but nobody seemed to know her address or even what last name she was going by now, and her girlfriend told me that the best thing to do would be forget it. "Don't sweat it, whiteboy. Just figure you been Negrofied, that's all," she said. "Happens in the best of families."

And, well, anyhow, I was dozing there on the steps down to the beach and having this light-sleep dream of being with Rosie again in our little bush house in the park— until, from some faraway place in like the geography of my memory dream, I heard some female screaming. At first I thought it was some kind of psychic phenomenon, like Rosie's soul reaching me from whatever faraway hellish ghetto she was in now, screaming invectives from her side of that colorline they kept between us. Then memory goosed my consciousness and I knew that couldn't be it— Rosie didn't scream in a highpitched screech, she hollered and yelled in a throaty contralto. And I opened my eyes to be dazzled by the patio, all a-sparkle under the bright morning sun.

I rubbed my eyes and came to my feet, and went at a jog toward the house to find out what new and interesting turn their party had taken now. And there in the main room were two girls—Cash and one of those who shall ever remain anonymous to me. This girl was rummaging through the mess trying to find her things and Cash was coming along after her, screaming like she'd lost her mind. "You bitch! You nasty little bitch! Ayeeee!" And whacking the girl with the bristled end of a broom. The girl took a few whacks on the back and butt, then she turned on

210

Cash, grabbed the end of the broom and yelled back: "Shut up and let me get *out* of here!" Then the two of them went waltzing around, each on one end of the broom, trying to wrestle it out of the hands of the other—till Cash tripped on some rubble and went down. The other girl tossed the broom as far away as she could, and went back to her search, and Cash got up and just stood there watching silently, a strange kind of silence with the girl scrunching around in the wreckage, mumbling to herself. Finally, she gave up the search and walked out the front door, and presently there was the roar of a car starting, then gravel being thrown from under the back wheels as she drove off.

Then a few more of them drifted downstairs and Cash went to a far corner of the main room and sat down on the floor, and watched as the first three of them searched through the mess for their overnight bags, pocketbooks, bathingsuits, waterskies, surfboards. Then the main room was filling up with them and a dozen or so were rummaging through the wreckage. Cash got up and went wandering like some kind of weary shrew, as if she wanted to hurt them but was too tired to try. She stopped wandering once long enough to shout, *"You'll* hear from me about this. You'll *hear* from me." But they paid no attention, just went on hunting, looking like a bunch of ragpickers, bent over, fingering this item and that. Most of the boys were shirtless and some were in their underwear shorts and stepping gingerly about on bare feet. A few of the girls came down the stairs bare bosomed and grabbed the first bra they found, and one came upon the scene bare bottomed to go crouching self-consciously over the first bag she came to and dig out a pair of shorts, tug them up and then go on looking for her own things.

Then there was more highpitched screeching, this time coming from the second floor, and I realized Cash had gone up there; she was chasing somebody downstairs, I could tell by the cries and the pounding feet, and here came the redhead with the ribbon still neatly tied in the top of her head, and behind her the guy who'd held batting practice on my balcony.

The phone rang but the hunters ignored it like it didn't exist, and from my balcony, Cash yelled down at them, "Don't answer that, don't any of you answer that." When she saw they weren't about to even hear it, she disappeared back into the bowels of the house and soon I heard the thumping of feet and more yelps as she chased down another couple—Judy and an elephantine elegant who was having trouble getting his pants zipped up.

Things were being located now and they were departing in quick succession. The way they were leaving was the way they'd arrived, alone or in pairs of girls, pairs of boys, to continue their trips home from college.

The muscular lifeguard, the guy who'd dived into the aquarium after the fisherman, came down the main stairs, viewed the wreckage, rubbed his eyes, yawned and walked off without hunting for anything—out to the patio he went, down the steps to the beach, down the beach and straight into the sea; he swam in a lazy crawl out to the yacht and pretty soon there came the purring of its engine and it moved off leaving a wake rippling the sea's glassy surface. As it did, a girl dashed out and went chasing down after it, waving frantically and calling for the guy to wait for

212

her, wait for her. But he didn't. She went all the way into the shallows before she gave it up and turned back, and as she walked past me into the main room she gave me about the dirtiest look I've ever gotten, as if she thought it was my fault she'd missed the boat.

I found my coffee cup, then, and went back for a refill; when I got back to my post on the patio just outside the smashed doors, Harry was among those hunting through the wreckage. As he rummaged about, Mary appeared from the stairs to the south wing, and she was still wearing that ridiculous hat with the long white feather. Then from under one of the overhangs, Cash ran out, snatched the hat from her head and stood there trying to rip it. She couldn't get a rip started, so she gave up tugging and found a piece of glass, and then she cut the hat to shreds, holding up piece after piece of it until it was all in bits. And by that time, Harry was on his way out the door and Mary was watching him go; he went without a backward glance.

Then I noticed Nancy-baby walking into the scene. She was very erect and gazing about at the others with a sort of snobbish expression. Her clothes—the ones I'd gotten her—were neatly intact; she looked too well dressed to have ever been one of them and I silently hoped as I watched that this was some sort of indication of what would become of her life. Me, you, everybody, she'd said —what's going to become of us? But didn't she know that for them there was no us? That the rationale of their lives was disunity, the takers and the took, the one of the *Shoulds* that had been built into them was that it's smart to be a taker and stupid to get took? Didn't she know that?

213

Well, Nancy'd been taken by them, and so had Cash. And so, finally, had practically all of them been taken by another of them, one way or another, for once they put the house-wrecking behind them they had used each other and been used—social ecology. And now I could see that they were feeling humiliated, most of them. It's their morals, I said to myself. But it's a new day and they'll soon be restored to their former state of Should and they'll go on living in it.

When the last of the strays came and went and Arnold wasn't among them, I began to get a bit worried; I finished my coffee and stepped inside. I was walking as quietly over the crunching glass as I could, peering this way and that, wondering if I should make a search of the house for him, when I heard an unlikely *swoosh*-rattle. And I stopped and turned and there in the dining area was the old man; he had a pushbroom and was sweeping everything toward the general pile in the main room. His face was the same expressionless mask it had been the afternoon before when he'd been out trimming the hedges in the midst of the partying.

It stopped me, his being up bright and early sweeping away like this; I stopped in my tracks and stared at him. To judge by his face and actions, it was as if this hor-rendous housewrecking that had gone on right outside his little apartment—as if all that had nothing to do with him—he wasn't one of them either. For himself, he seemed to be saying, it was enough that this morning he had work to do, and by tonight he would have done some of it, and what more could a man ask. Maybe this reading was all wrong, for surely it was my own; maybe behind that stern brow and billygoat goatee he was absolutely horrified by

214

what he was confronting this morning—or maybe delighted, who knows? But seeing him there so coolly pushing his broom along, absorbing himself in this work that was right before him and ignoring the rest of the tangle and havoc, concentrating strictly on this first of his many tasks —the sight of this snapped me out of my morning lethargy, made me forget everything else and put me sitting on a step, watching him work. And listening—listening hard into the rattle of broomed glass, the chirpings of morning birds, the roar and pounding of the surf—all these new sounds of this new day.

Cash was standing there in the middle of the rubble, just standing there with her head down and I thought she must be in some sad depression; her shoulders were shaking and it looked like she was sobbing. Until she turned slightly and then I saw her face—she was standing in the middle of this mess shaking with silent laughter.

Now she moved about, inspecting this bit of rubble and that splinter of glass. Soul-satisfied or horrified into nuttiness, I couldn't tell which, but she looked secretly delighted by it all. She found a figurine that was still together and she picked it up and turned it over in her hand. Then she gave a girlish wind-up and pitched it at the wall. It bonked and fell, still intact. So she picked up a piece of statue—an arm with elbow slightly bent—and used this as a club and managed to disintegrate the figurine.

When she turned away from this, she had a cruel and gleeful look in her eye—until she noticed me sitting on the steps. Then the expression drained from her and she went pale. *"You* still here!"

She picked up the base of a broken vase and, like a child

215

throwing a tantrum, she smashed it to the floor; it exploded into fragments. And like this act had helped her get control of herself, she looked at me now with put-on composure. "Don't you think," she said in her usual clipped and even speech, "it's time you *left?*"

I allowed as how it was and picked myself up and was scrunching through the puddle of wet wreckage toward the door. It looked like everyone else had gone, including Arnold. So I was trying to resign myself to a long walk back to the highway and hoping to catch a ride from there back to the university—when I encountered the stone form of the nude Athenian girl laid out on her back beside the armor of the gone knight. And with something like a reflex action, I bent down and picked up the knight and went carrying him with me. I took him to his place just inside the front door and tried to stand him up, but one of his legs was missing and so was his lance, and I turned back to look for them. I spotted the missing leg right away—draped over a podium—but the lance took some hunting, so I roamed around, carrying the leg with me.

There was something sticking up out of the ooze at the bottom of the aquarium—which turned out to be the end of the knight's lance. Someone had speared the ooze with it.

Back to their knight I went with these, passing Cash, still standing in the middle of the mess and looking at me now with plain curiosity. I tried to put the knight back together but I couldn't get the leg to stay under him, so I put the whole works down in a neat pile where he'd stood. This bit of work was giving me a strange twinge of delight and I was about to turn for more when some-

216

thing struck the wall near my head and clattered to the floor. She'd pitched a piece of something at me.

"Have a *ball!*" she demanded. "Break *every*thing! Don't leave *any*thing unbroken!" And as if to illustrate her point, she began moving around, kicking, picking things up and throwing them down, her skirt billowing and twisting like she was doing some wild kind of dance.

Well, I watched this action a moment, then turned back to my restoration work. And when I did, she sort of wound down, went and sat on a step and watched me.

I found the face of a Roman I remembered from somewhere, and near that I found most of his neck—it fit up under his chin. Then I sloshed around in the mess looking for the rest of him. For quite a while I hunted and she watched, and I was feeling caught between her curious, sullen gaze and the swooshing and rattling of the caretaker's sweeping. And I was finding that, like the old man so absorbed in his task, I was becoming absorbed in mine. But I wasn't finding the rest of this Roman, so I took what I had of him and walked over to Cash and held the stone face in front of her eyes and asked, "Who's this?"

She turned her face away like she was too disgusted to even think about it, but I shoved the stone face in front of her eyes again. "Who's this?"

"Nero," she groaned. "Is that supposed to be appropriate?"

"Where does Nero go?"

"None of your business. Put it down."

But then I remembered. "Ah. At the top of the stairs. That's where Nero was, isn't it."

So I took what I had of him and went upstairs to the

217

pedestal where Nero had perched. And as I was coming back down the stairs, she said, "Just what do you think you are doing?"

I didn't know exactly. Hadn't stopped to think about it. I guessed—now that she mentioned it—that I was going about this restoration business just to delay the long walk back to the highway. So I said, "I'm putting Nero back together again."

"Well, *please*. Don't *bother*."

"It's no bother. I'm enjoying it."

"Really!" she said, snide and flippant. "You enjoyed yourself last night too. Didn't you?"

I pretended I hadn't heard and went on hunting.

"I saw you up there—*laughing!"*

I didn't remember laughing and was about to say so when she burst into laughter. "Junk," she squealed. "You came in here calling everything junk. *Junk!"* Like she was trying to make a joke out of it, but her laughter was coming in gags and her bosom was heaving, like she was confusing laughing with crying. "Well, that's what it is! Now! Junk is just what you *made* it. Oh my god! Junk. Ah ha ha ha."

"Hey, what's all this crap about? *I* made it! Listen, bitch, I'm the only one of your guests that did *not* help wreck this place. Now why are you trying to say it's *my* fault? What the hell do you think I did—*spook* everybody into it?"

"That's what you did!" she shouted like she'd just made a discovery. "That's it! You *spook,* you!"

Which caused me to drawl: "Ma'am, Ah'd like t'take credit, Ah really would. Only thing is, I wasn't the only spice in the stew. What about *you?* Now you's the one invited ever'body into yore house. Right? This great big

218

mothafuckin' house fulla shitcovered *things*. Where nobody *lives*. Where some old people takes *care,* and a cat
chases mice."

She sat looking up at me with a supercilious grin.

"Then," I said, moving toward her, "you made a great
big deal out of trying to keep everybody away. From everything—you tried to keep them away from Nancy, and you
tried to keep them away from your daddy's precious *things.*
Hey, baby, you wanna know what I think? I think you
de*fended* the idea right into their *heads.* You defended them
into the gangbang and you defended them into this, and
you—"

She was crawling up the stairs now—crawling on all
fours like a frightened animal. Glancing back over her
shoulder at me with something like terror in her eyes. But
even this action was some kind of phoniness, for she crawled
up half a dozen steps and let herself slide back four, then
went to crawling up again, as if she was frantic to get away
from me, as if she thought I was about to—

And I found myself moving after her, like I was being
drawn by her fear. Now we were moving in fits and starts
—each time I made a move toward her, she gave a terrified
little whimper and scrambled up a few more steps, and
each time I stopped, she slumped and lay on the stairs staring back at me, waiting.

Well, I knew just what was happening—she was provok-
ing it. And in some part of my mind I was trying to tell
myself not to let her do this to me. Yet she was suggesting
a keen lust right into my loins—defending me into going
after her.

Near the top of the stairs I lunged for her and she

219

sprang to her feet and ran a short way down the hall. Then she huddled against the wall, letting out little cries of horror. And when I moved toward her, she ran further down the hall and stopped, turned and made more sounds of horror. She reached the room she'd taken me to earlier and darted into it, then poked her head out and said, "Don't you *dare!*"

Like she thought I was what they call the Communist Menace. This whole bit she was going through was an act, so phony. It was like her way of demanding it, pulling me into it.

As I walked toward her, I said, "You're some funny chick."

"Stay away!"

"This is how you did it—how you caused it to happen."

"No! You're *insane!* Don't come *near* me!"

When I got to the door, she pulled her head in, and when I went into the room she was on the bed, laying on her back, propped up on her elbows, legs spread, watching me move toward her like she thought I was carrying a knife and was about to cut her to ribbons. I felt like saying, Okay, come off the horror act now and get out of your clothes. But she was living her act—she was so full of fear I could smell it like rising up out of her pores, and as if it were some kind of intoxicating perfume, it had me playing the role she expected. I picked up the front of her skirt and tossed it up over her face, then I yanked her pants off and threw them into a corner, dropped my pants and underwear to my ankles and got onto the bed between her legs, pushing her further onto it so our legs wouldn't be hanging over the side.

The hem of her skirt slid off her face as I pushed and she was grimacing at me now, scowling and tight-lipped with some kind of horror and indignation she really did believe she felt. But as soon as the head of my cock touched the lips of her cunt, she fell back hissing in her breath, and as I pressed into her she closed her eyes and her mouth came open. It was a very greedy and self-centered lust she had, for quickly now she was going for herself with the nervous, trembly motions of the needy. It was making such a gigolo out of me—such a tool and a fool—but I couldn't help it, I just naturally responded to her need. Prince Randy, I said to myself, what a benevolent oaf you are! And why can't *they* respond like this? Then I thought of their Shoulds and for an instant I was on top of hating her, feeling tempted to pull out of her greedy, needful cunt, hoist her legs and shove it up her ass—sodomy with social overtones. But my hate didn't stand a chance, for her need had me trapped and I was catering to her particular poverty, reaching into those nervous, trembling motions, while she made her raid on the goodies her Shoulds had forbidden, like a frightened jewel thief at the Waldorf-Astoria. When she started to come, she let out little shouts —something between panic and joy. I raised my head to see her expression—the usually tight, grim lips now in the shape of an O, and the eyes glazed, staring past me like I wasn't there. Then I felt her vibrations as she made it to her satisfaction and I put my head down and went for myself. I made it to mine as she was coming down from hers, and I made it none too soon, for a moment later she was pushing my shoulders, trying to get me off her.

I rolled and lay beside her, thinking, Well now, richbitch, it sure would be something if you decided to call this rape. And like I was hearing sounds I only imagined, I heard, "You raped me!"

"Wow!" was all I could think to say. She lay beside me with her face turned away.

"You raped me!" she repeated.

"Roll over and I'll do it again."

"You *beast!*"

Which hurt my right ear, for she'd turned to me and yelped that with her mouth an inch from my face.

I got up and pulled up my shorts and pants and was zipping my fly when she said, "What are you going to do *now?*"

"Wow," I said, wondering what *she* was going to do now—provoke me into setting fire to the whole house?

"I'm leaving."

"Get out!" she ordered.

"You're some funny chick."

"Shut up and get out."

"I'm on my way."

And I was, but at the top of the stairs I was halted, for down there in the midst of the rubble was a middle-aged man dressed in a business suit. He was standing there surveying the wreckage, and from behind me came Cash's stage whisper: "Oh my God! Daddy!"

I went back into the shelter of the hall and stood beside her as she peeked over the railing and watched her father, as he strolled through the mess in his shiny leather shoes. And now *I* was scared. Randy boy, I said to myself, there's gonna be hell t'pay if this crazy richbitch runs down there and tells her daddy it's all your fault, that you wrecked his house and raped his daughter. That could lead to bad, bad trouble—considering who he is and who you are.

And I was standing behind her thinking this when she turned around, lifted an arm and pointed toward the stairs, and like a stiff-backed playground instructor said, *"Out!"* Then she took off at a quick clip for the stairs and I followed, and down we came to confront her daddy.

Who was . . . well, imagine an old duff who'd name a daughter Cash. He brought that sort of spirit into the room. Jowly, bald, pink old buzzard who looked nothing like her. Standing there with his head lifting and turning this way and that, checking the damage.

As we marched down the stairs, she was saying, "Daddy! Oh Daddy!" But he was oblivious to her—he just stood there looking at the wreckage, and when we got to the bottom of the stairs and I saw the expression on his face, *I* was astounded. *He* wasn't! It was like all this horrendous havoc that was meeting his eye was moving him not at all.

Cash was confused too. But she found a cop-out—she turned on me and said, "Came in here, fingering everything . . ." And she went into a pantomime of how I'd done this fingering of things when I'd first arrived here— she had a hand on her hip and was lifting imaginary sheets with the other hand and making slapping motions in the air, like trying to tell her father, who was watching her now, whose fault it was that all this had happened. "As if," she said to me, "you thought all this was *yours!* To either *like* it or des*troy* it!"

I opened my mouth to say something, anything—even go along with this act she was putting on. But before I could stammer something, she rushed up to me and hollered into my face: *"Idiot!* It wasn't even mine! *Nor* my father's."

"Who," I finally managed, "owns it—er, *owned* it?"

"Who owned it! Don't you understand? You don't *own* something like this, you take *care* of it and pass it *on."*

I was so surprised to hear *her* say this that I was speechless; I glanced at her father, who was watching me, waiting like a judge at a trial.

"Did I *hear* you right?" I tried. "You take care of it and pass it on?"

"Yes," she hissed, and stood there staring at me hard, and we were locked eyeball to eyeball.

"Yes *but!"* I bit at her, and was tempted to take off on a tirade, like, You richbitch, you and your kind take care of this the same way you do our labor, our ingenuity, we of the lowlies—us ignorant, shiftless, immoral no-accounts who made what you got papers say you own. You either keep it all to yourselves or throw us a crumb and call it a give-away, you benevolent bastards. Well, fuck this fine museum you buried in shit way out here in the middle of nowhere—it's as ruined as you are now. Do the world a favor and *don't* pass anything on. Bury yourself in it.

But I didn't say a thing. Just stood locked in this eye-to-eye stance with her until I heard her father moving about.

He'd given up waiting for our debate to continue and was going around, like making mental notes. Seeing what had happened and analyzing it, I guess. Maybe making an accounting of what had been completely destroyed and what could be salvaged. And he seemed, still, not at all

224

upset. Like he'd known all along that this lesser Metropolitan Museum in the wilds was doomed to be wrecked somehow, someday, and now that it had happened his main concern was analyzing it, methodically.

"Daddy," she was saying, "oh Daddy! I'm sick, I'm absolutely sick! I can't *tell* you—I just can't begin to describe what went on here last night. It's *too awful!*"

But he paid no attention to her. He was as unmoved by the sounds she was making as he was by the sights he was seeing. He looked like a tired tourist strolling around an ancient ruin, and his lack of reaction had me so overwhelmed that I was just gaping at him, flabbergasted.

Until Cash, like some amateur actress playing Medea on pep pills, stretched out her arm and pointed a stiff finger at me and choked: *"Him!* Daddy, get him *out* of here."

And without even glancing at me he lifted his arm and made a lazy waving motion toward the door.

I left. Walked outside into a day as clear as the proverbial bell, a blinding sun in a sky of deep blue, and I was heading toward the gate out of this blasted baronial beautification, was even beginning to look forward to that long walk back to the highway because I knew it would relax me and I was all wound up tight. When, out of the corner of my eye, I saw Arnold's little MG. Bright and sassy beside her father's big Cadillac. And there was Arnold, stretched out on the lawn beside it, asleep in the morning sun.

I had half a mind to leave him there and go it alone by foot. I was in no mood for any of his pontifical nonsense, but if he had waited for me, I figured, the least I could do was acknowledge it. So I went over and nudged him

225

with my foot and when he opened his eyes, I cracked, "Now I don't care whether you had your dessert or not, let's get the hell out of here."

He got up and staggered to the shotgun seat and tossed me the keys, and as I was getting in behind the wheel I noticed the lump on his head. A big red goose egg on his forehead. I pointed to it and said, "What's that?"

"Harry," he yawned.

"He hit you instead of loved you, eh."

"No, that's *not* it."

"Well, what happened?"

"Dunderhead, nobody loves anybody else. I'm convinced of it—we all love what we think we are in relation to someone else."

"Well? That doesn't explain that lump."

"He's a tortured prig!"

"Did he catch you and beat you up?"

"No! I found him and completed my masterplan."

"Wow! The last time I saw him, he was out to kill you."

"Well . . . I found him and he changed his mind. It was right after he'd followed me into the delights of the no-longer-virgin Mary, you see. We talked awhile. I tried to explain the facts of life to him, and I did, of course, indicate how much I admired him, and he went with me down to the girls' changing room."

"Um."

"Yes. But then, you see—after everything had gone so *beauti*fully . . . and oh my, dunderhead, he is *so* magnificent —oh, oh, *oh!*"

"Yeah, sure. And *then?*"

"Well, then—I don't have the slightest idea, really. All

226

I know is, he hit me, pounded on me with his fists and he cried like a baby. Chased me around in there trying to hit me some more. I mean, he let me *have* him and then he *hit* me! Think of it, dunderhead, he hit me like I'm the torture inside his stupid, priggish brain."

"It could have been worse," I warned.

"They're all so *stup*id! But enough of that. Tell me—"

"Don't ask."

"Yes, tell me what became of you."

"Cash raped me."

"Wonderful!" he said, and straightened up in his seat. "Listen, you goof, she'll make a fine ride to the thin air. Yes she will. Beautiful! I'm so happy to hear everything worked out. One of these days, you oaf, you'll be one of *us.*"

I drove on in silence, for that put my emotions into a state of confusion, like a popcorn maker full of kernels of joy, kernels of sorrow. One moment I was popping a thought that almost gagged me with laughter, the next I was deep in the tomb of some sad and funky realizations. One of these days I would *not* be one of his us, and one of these days I would have to tell him. In the meantime, I had to get used to it—I wasn't going to make it to the olympics, and I'd lost my ambition to have a daughter of the newmoney who has those certain guilts. Smashed, that ambition, just as surely as the contents of that house we were leaving behind us as I drove that MG hellbent for the highway. And I'd have to break the news to him, one of these days—that he could fix me up with one-more-chances till the cows came home, but it wouldn't work. Never.

But I put off telling him—he slept and I drove, and

I relished my feelings. For I was feeling like a man who's been toting a wounded friend across a desert, trudging along with this heavy weight on his back. And, like he just found out his friend is dead, that he'd been carrying a corpse. Well, it's a sad thing to find he's gone—you'll miss him, you'll grieve for him. But on the other hand, you're much lighter now, and now you can move on without the burden, travel much faster.

And, well, before we reached the city, I'd had a funeral for those old and cherished ambitions, had practically forgotten them. I was surprised how well they died.

Arnold didn't wake up till I stopped the car in front of his apartment building, then he stretched, yawned, and said, "So, you see, dunderhead, the party was a success after all."

"Yes," I said, "it sure enough was."

18

THAT WAS THE FIRST and last I ever saw of them, that particular covy of the sons and daughters of the rich and powerful. I left the university for the summer and never went back again, which did cause my friendship with Arnold to cool a bit, for it put us going separate ways.

But we still see each other once in a while. He's concentrating these days on getting the lock's tumblers—certain combinations of his father's associates—to fall into place so he can open some controlroom, one of the pilothouses of our various states of pomp and chaos, and run things. I figure he'll make it, sooner or later. And, knowing him, I like to imagine what will happen when he does.

He comes down here to see me every so often, to tell me of his progress and hint that I am missing all sorts of good things in life by being such a complete dropout, by making a career out of staying here at this motel on the coast where I am what they call a beachboy. But it's a very good life, all things considered; I wouldn't trade it for any other I know of. I get to develop my fascination with the rich and powerful, for it's a fashionable and exclusive motel I'm at. And when they come down here from their more rarefied heights, come practically naked padding out to the pool or beach, they are stepping onto *my* turf, and I take great pleasure in planting little seeds in their psyches while they're here.

I own the pool and beach concession here. It's not an enterprise that violates my sense of social justice by threatening to enrich my heirs; it's just a little piece of this old earth that I have, and only for the time being; it's for me to make a living from, and that's any mortal's rightful share, I figure.

A good many of the rich and powerful who come here have heard about Cash's party; that's why I still meet some who ask why it happened. Who say they could understand kids from the slums behaving that way, but the sons and daughters of our best families—why them?

Which, as I said up front, I don't try to answer. Sometimes I tell them *what* happened, or part of it. But I never, never venture into the *who* or the unscrewable inscrutable of *why* it happened. And if they persist in picking at me to come up with some theory, I check my watch and suddenly remember I have something urgent to attend to.

And that's a joke on them too, for there's no longer anything urgent about my life. Nowadays I think of myself as one of us, the all-pervasive us, and the only ambition I harbor now is for the high noon of the infinite is, the midnight of the oversoul. Because I'm no longer reduced to either fighting them or joining them; I'm no longer prejudiced against them either. Prejudice is a form of envy and I can't possibly feel envy for them, for I've had a postparty premonition of what is most likely to become of them—the dollar-glutted, automated deadend where they soon will have achieved such glots of profit they'll simply

230

become like cancerous cells—and I'm content to play it cool, to wait and watch it happen.

I am still, you see, the poorboy at their party, spooking them. And hoping that, next time around, the rest of us will find a way to make the benefits of our earth—our work, beauty, ingenuity—count for us all instead of whoring it away and putting some other them at a deadend.